TAURUS

21st April – 20th May

A new friendship is on the horizon but be cautious – things may not be all that they seem. The past may come back to haunt someone close to you and there might be unpleasant events ahead.

Also available in this series

MARIA PALMER

HORRORSCOPES

TAURUS

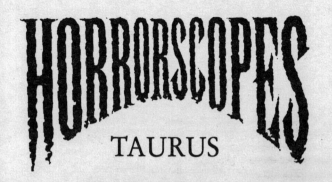

MIRROR IMAGE

MAMMOTH

First published in Great Britain 1995
by Mammoth, an imprint of Reed Books Ltd
Michelin House, 81 Fulham Road, London SW3 6RB
and Auckland, Melbourne, Singapore and Toronto

Reprinted 1995

Copyright © Dave Morris, 1995

The right of Dave Morris to be identified as author of this
work has been asserted by him in accordance with
the Copyright, Designs and Patents Act 1988

Horrorscopes is a trademark of Reed International Books Ltd

ISBN 0 7497 1885 4

A CIP catalogue record for this title
is available from the British Library

Printed and bound in Great Britain
by Cox & Wyman Ltd, Reading, Berkshire

ONE

I remember when Jeanette came to the school as clearly as if it were yesterday. How could I forget it? With her came the most evil I have ever known in my life.

I don't think that she herself was evil. But it streamed in with her, like a cold wind following someone through an open door. It came in and swirled around us all, leaving a chill on all it touched.

Of course I registered that a new girl had arrived – you always do, especially if she appears the day after half-term. Jeanette Skelton was petite, dark-haired, with the kind of well-defined, almost oriental features I always wish I had. She seemed very quiet at first.

When school finished the bus was late, as usual. I spent a bored ten minutes with nothing to read but a magazine I found at the bus stop. I glanced through my horoscope with a half-sceptical eye. It said something about new friendships and I promptly forgot it until later. Finally I was walking down the lane from the bus stop to my house, and gradually became aware of a figure wandering uncertainly towards me, huddled against the February wind. She came closer and I saw it was Jeanette. She stopped by the crossroads of Sandy Drive and Applewood Gardens, and looked from one to the other as if trying to make up her mind where to go next.

I walked up to her. 'Need some help?' I said.

She turned round with a relieved smile. 'Could you tell me how to get to Oakhill Rise? I just moved to the area and I'm afraid I'm rather lost.' Her voice was quiet and had a soft accent I didn't recognise.

'These roads are like a warren,' I replied. 'Oakhill is on my way home – why don't you walk with me?' She looked even more relieved, which made her seem very young, although I'd guess she was about my age. 'By the way, I'm Dianne Woods.'

'Jeanette Skelton,' she replied as we set off.

'Didn't you start at Manor Gate School today?' She nodded.

'It's a bit unusual to start in the middle of term, isn't it?'

'It's a long story,' said Jeanette, pulling a face. 'Basically my parents would have moved here much earlier. Last October they inherited a house that's been in the family for about a hundred years, but it took ages to sort out the death duties.'

'So you're living in a place full of creaky floorboards and portraits of your ancestors?'

She laughed shyly. 'No, it's quite normal really. Disappointingly so. And no paintings, I'm afraid. Just some creaky old antiques.'

'Still, it must be pretty amazing to live some-where that's got a family history.'

'You mean knowing that every mark and stain has been made by a Skelton?' she laughed. 'My mother doesn't think so. She's decided we're not to have any visitors until she's changed everything.'

'What a drag,' I said.

We chatted easily and by the time we were at Oakhill I decided I rather liked her. I waved goodbye to her at her door – and, yes, it was a perfectly normal-looking house.

The next day at school I introduced Jeanette prop-erly to my best friend, Jill Casey. She had this terrific figure and neat blonde bobbed hair, which I envied, although she always said she wished she had my red mane. And I introduced Jeanette to Benedict Knight, who also hung around with us.

I'd known him on and off since the first year, when he was spotty and small with grazes on his knees. It was strange to remember him like that when in fact he had grown quite tall. I was marvelling at the transformation more and more. His dark tousled hair, however, still hadn't been tamed. We had only become good friends that term, which was surprising, as we discovered we had a lot in common. Ben had always been shy and self-effacing – quite different from other guys. Perhaps that's why I liked him so much; that and his considerate nature and sensitivity.

The first thing Ben said to Jeanette when he met her was: 'Do you like swimming?'

'Don't go dragging her up and down that pool for hours,' I said. 'I know what you and Jill are like.'

'Ignore Di, she's just strange,' said Jill.

'I just don't like getting water up my nose and in my ears. I end up feeling sick. I prefer my exercise to be less messy – like taking the dog for a walk. Anyway,' I added, well into my stride, 'chlorine dries out your hair and skin.'

'Not if you use conditioner and moisturiser,' said Jill.

'Well, Jeanette, do you feel like bringing your beauty aids along for a dip at swimming club tonight?' asked Ben.

'Actually, I'd rather like to,' she replied, with a slight blush. 'Thank you very much.'

So we took Jeanette under our wing and she began to come out of her shell. In biology one day Ben and Jill had managed to grab the back bench so that we could sit as a foursome. Jeanette and I were a little late and they waved madly at us to join them before someone else got our places. The teacher, Mrs Molnar, came in and demanded our attention, so I didn't notice what Jeanette was doing until Ben nudged me.

Behind the benches is a large fish tank, which at that time was home to a large and beautiful angel fish. In bored moments I would tap the glass and watch it dart from side to side, its face wearing a permanently startled expression. Then it would tire of our game and scoot off to the other side of the tank.

4

It seemed that Jeanette shared my fascination for the creature. She was staring into the tank as if mesmerised, watching the fish glide around as if she was looking deep into a crystal ball.

I elbowed Jill gently and she had a quick glance. 'Ah,' she said. 'Another sister in fish-watching.' We both giggled and then thought we'd better pay attention to the lesson. Soon we were told to get out our practical books and collect some equipment.

'Hey,' said Jill, amid the sound of scraping chairs. 'Where's the fish gone?'

Ben and I turned around and looked. We all looked. We couldn't see it anywhere.

'Maybe it's dug a burrow,' said Ben, and tapped the tank. Nothing moved. 'Or had a heart attack?' He turned back around.

Jeanette was sitting with a serene expression on her face. She shook her head and licked her lips, exactly like a cat.

We couldn't help it, we all cracked up with laughter – and instantly earned a reprimand from Mrs Molnar. Jill and I sobered up but Ben kept bursting into fresh fits whenever he looked at Jeanette.

Actually the fish never did come back and it wasn't ever found dead in the tank either, despite a mini-inquest from the school.

The next lesson Jill and I had a free period.

'Library?' said Jill. I nodded and fell into step beside her. 'Sam's coming to Carla's sixteenth at the weekend,' she said. 'Y'know, I think you should ask Ben.'

My heart gave a little flutter of excitement, which I quickly tried to be sensible about and ignore. 'He's already invited. He can go with anyone he likes.'

Jill leaned close and said in a low voice, 'And I think you'd like it if he went with you.'

I stared at her. 'Oh God, is it that obvious that I'm interested in him?'

She gave me a knowing look. 'Only to your nearest and dearest,' she smiled. 'Particularly after the way you were keeping a close eye on how he was looking at Jeanette.'

I felt myself blush to the roots. 'Oh no, was I?'

'You and Ben would make a good couple,' she said, ignoring my embarrassment.

'We're just friends,' I replied. 'He's not ever going to see me as anything but that. Besides, I'm just not interesting enough. I don't do funny things like Jeanette does.'

'It's not a good thing to start getting jealous,' she said with a mischievous twinkle in her eye.

'I'm not,' I said, a little more seriously than she was being. 'I just know my limitations.'

All the same I wished I wasn't so aware of them. I wished I was wacky and spontaneous like Jeanette. How ironic.

'Hi, am I late?'

Jeanette was standing in front of me wearing a voluminous raincoat. It was Saturday and I was going to show her the best shops, as she hadn't got a thing to wear to Carla's party. I had been waiting for Jeanette in the coffee shop for about five minutes.

'No, not at all,' I said, jumping up. I noticed the fine spray of water on her coat. 'Is it raining?'

'Not at the moment, although I think there's a storm brewing.'

I peered out of the window. The sky looked a bit dark, but not exactly angry. 'We could chance it.'

She smiled diffidently. 'I don't mind if you don't mind.' She was so easy-going and calm in those days.

'Well, we have to find you something to wear,' I said, and led the way out of the shop.

So we set off. First we looked at the stores and I helped her choose some earrings that looked really great against her blue-black hair. It was rather fun to search out things that might suit her, as her colouring was totally different from mine. When Jill and I went shopping we usually found the same things looked good on us, but with Jeanette it felt like more of an adventure.

But after all our research we still couldn't find a dress that Jeanette liked. We ended up staring in the window of Nickell's department store for inspiration.

'Do we dare go in here?' said Jeanette, looking in astonishment at some of the prices.

There was a rumble of thunder. 'No,' I said, 'but I think we'll have to shelter under the awning until this passes.'

There was another rumble and the rain started

7

to fall, loudly and aggressively. Jeanette moved along to another window to look at some shoes.

I turned back to take another look at the jewellery near the clothes. The wind threw the rain against my back. And then I saw a strange thing – Jeanette, there in the shop window. Her face. No one else had features like that. But the expression wasn't like hers at all. It was twisted and cruel.

I waved at her, hoping to see her face relax into smiles again. But she carried on staring ahead in that horrible way. I waved again, but I had to look away because I felt too unnerved. And then I saw her, two windows down, absorbed in looking at shoes, her face happy and contented.

I turned back to my window. The other Jeanette was still in there. As I watched, she turned on her heel and seemed – literally – to vanish.

I suppose it must have been a trick of the light. Some of those windows have reflective coatings and you can see some quite odd effects. But actually I'd never seen one that eerie. I tried to look for any other strange effects, but didn't find any. And then the storm passed.

Jeanette wandered back from her window. Should I say anything about my little experience? Then the sun came out for the first time that day and the mood passed.

'We'd better find somewhere else to shop before we acquire some expensive tastes,' I said.

At last we found an outfit Jeanette liked. It was a short white skirt with a navy and white striped T-shirt and it looked great against her midnight-coloured hair and long slim limbs. I'm more stocky, although I'm not fat. Actually I remember reading that my figure is a typical Taurean shape. But I managed to find a really nice green narrow skirt in the same shop, so we both came out pretty pleased.

Later we were walking back down Applewood Gardens when I saw a figure in the distance with a pushchair and a golden Labrador.

'That's Mum and Charlie and Bubbles,' I said to Jeanette. 'I guess I'd better introduce you.'

We caught up with them and I introduced Jeanette to Mum, my little brother Charlie, and the Labrador, Bubbles. I remember Bubbles didn't seem exactly keen on Jeanette, which I thought was odd, as he was usually quite friendly.

'Pleased to meet you,' said Mum.

Jeanette bent down to say hello to Charlie. 'How old is he?'

'Two and a half,' replied Mum proudly. 'Have you got any brothers or sisters?'

'No,' replied Jeanette, straightening up.

'So you're an only child,' she said. I wish parents wouldn't state the obvious to keep a conversation going. 'That must be a bit lonely.'

'Well, I've never known anything else,' said Jeanette politely.

'Did your parents want any other children?' Mum asked.

I glared at her to tell her stop asking silly questions but she didn't seem to notice. 'Not everyone wants a big family,' I muttered.

9

'Actually,' said Jeanette, 'my parents were convinced I was going to be a boy because on my father's side no one ever had girls.'

'Really?' said Mum. 'How unusual.'

'My mother said it's because the girls in his family tend to be cursed.'

I laughed and Mum looked confused for a moment before joining in too. She's never quite known what to make of my friends' wacky sense of humour.

Jeanette's remark seemed to put the nail in the coffin of that conversation, to my relief. She said she'd better be off home.

'Are you sure you don't want me to pick you up for the party later?' I said.

Jeanette nodded. 'I'll be fine. I think I know my way around now. I'll see you there at half-seven.'

'OK, see you later,' I called, and she set off for Oakhill.

'She seems a nice girl,' said Mum.

'Mmm,' I responded. Mum always said that. I'm sure she would even if I brought Lucrezia Borgia home for tea.

'I'm just on my way to the corner shop,' she said. 'Come with me and give me a hand.'

I took Bubbles' lead from her and nearly got towed away. The dog knew he had to behave with Mum but with me he expected an energetic, exciting walk. With some difficulty I calmed him down.

A little further down the road we met Mrs Hughes, who lives a couple of doors away. She's dotty about kids and always makes a fuss of Charlie. She bent down to give him a proper greeting and suddenly straightened up again with a stifled scream.

'What's that in his hands?' Her voice came out as a muffled squeak.

Mum and I were instantly on our knees in front of Charlie.

Behind us Mrs Hughes was taking deep breaths. 'I'm sorry, I can't touch it,' she gasped. 'Where on earth did he get a thing like that?'

Mum had snatched it away immediately, staring at the object in horror. 'I didn't see him pick this up.'

'I don't think he had it when Jeanette and I met you,' I managed to say. 'Jeanette would surely have noticed it. He must have picked it up off the street somewhere.'

'What a sick thing to leave lying around,' Mrs Hughes managed to stammer.

We looked at the object in Mum's hands. It was a large jam jar, almost boiling over with furious wasps. Charlie had been caught just as he was about to get the lid off.

TWO

It's lucky that Mum is a fairly level-headed person. Although she was shaken by finding the jar of wasps she couldn't think of any sensible explanation beyond the one that Charlie must have picked it up while we were distracted by something else – perhaps my attempts to restrain Bubbles. I don't know if she told Dad about it, or my older brother Mark.

Jill and Sam came around for me at around seven to take me to the party. Sam hung around downstairs while Jill and I had a crisis over choosing a suitable top to go with my new skirt.

Jill sat down on the bed, being careful not to crease her maroon velvet dress. 'So,' she said, eyes glittering with anticipation. 'Did you ask Ben?'

I gave her a withering look. 'You know I didn't.' I held up a couple of black tops.

Jill considered for a moment. 'The see-through, with the black sleeveless T-shirt you're wearing. You should have, you know. He wants you to – I can see it.'

I gave a sardonic smile. 'The trouble with you happy couples is that you want to see everybody else paired off. And you think it's so easy to do.'

'It is easy,' she said firmly.

I pulled on the see-through black blouse and tied the ends at the waist. 'If he wanted to go out with me he'd have said. He wouldn't have waited all this time. Sam asked you out straight away.'

'Sam's just got a different way of doing things,' replied Jill, standing up.

'Anyway,' I said, 'if I asked Ben he would probably be too nice to refuse. I don't want it to be like that.'

'Rubbish,' said Jill. 'You know it won't be. Ready?'

I hesitated for a moment. In the cosy atmosphere of my bedroom I had been about to tell her about the incident with the jar of wasps, but then decided not to because I was suddenly keen to get going. 'Ready as anything,' I said.

We joined Sam, who was looking pretty good in smart jeans and a shirt. As he and Jill walked ahead, arm in arm, I felt a surge of envy. It was so easy for them. They had got over the initial stage of awkwardness, of having to interpet signs and getting them wrong. Was it too late for me to start getting close to Ben? Even if he was interested, how would I get close to him?

I carried on wondering about this until we arrived at his house and he came bounding out, looking handsome in black jeans.

'I've got to be back by eleven,' he said ruefully. 'My parents have been nagging me to go to Mass

13

and confession with them tomorrow.' He gave Jill and me a hug each. In the face of such impartiality I sternly told myself to stop fantasising.

We got to Carla's house. The music was already quite loud. From the outside we could hear the volume surge and then die down, as people kept turning it up and others would turn it back down again. Inside smelled of perfumes and aftershaves, and the air in the kitchen contained the unmistakable tang of wine. I wondered if Carla's parents knew about that.

We left our coats in a pile in the front room and went to give our presents to Carla. She looked as if she was having a great time, her blonde hair had been done with curling tongs and she looked about nineteen. Practically everyone from our year must have been there, with a partner. Was I the only wallflower, I wondered mournfully – and then told myself to snap out of it.

'Let's go and find Jeanette,' said Ben. After a quick trip around the rooms that were being used for the party we couldn't see her.

'What time did she say she was coming?' asked Jill.

'Seven-thirty,' I replied.

Sam looked at his watch. 'It's nearly eight.'

'Maybe she got lost?' said Ben.

'She said she knew her way here,' I said.

As we spoke the doorbell went. Carla's brother went to open it. Then he called out, 'Carla, you didn't say this was fancy dress, did you?'

14

Intrigued, we stuck our heads around the lounge door to get a better look.

Jeanette came smoothly in through the door, wearing a dress that must have come out of the Ark.

'Is that what you went shopping for this afternoon?' hissed Jill in astonishment.

I shook my head vehemently. 'No. We bought a striped top and a white skirt.'

'Perhaps she spilled something on them,' said Jill.

Jeanette was walking slowly down the hallway. People were stepping aside as she went past, staying silent until they thought she was out of earshot. I heard a few titters.

'Come on,' I said to Jill. 'We'd better go and rescue her.'

But Jeanette didn't seem to be in need of rescuing. I don't think I'd ever seen anyone with such confidence as she had that night. It came off her like radiation. The dress was long, almost fish-tailed at the back. It was made of black velvet, so old that the pile had started going in various different directions, making it look as though the fabric was living skin that was part way through moulting. Looking more closely I definitely saw cobwebs hanging off one shoulder. But she didn't seem to care.

As she walked, the dress moved to reveal court shoes with toes so pointed they were like black arrows. Her face was plastered with white foundation, dusted with a pale powder, which made her already small features look even tinier. She was wearing very red lipstick and hardly any eye make-up. Her hair was scraped back into a severe bun.

I went up to her. 'Jeanette! You look – '

'Stunning,' said Ben, saving my blushes as I tried to tell a white lie and couldn't.

Seeing that Jeanette did actually know some people in the room, the watching crowds gradually turned back to their own friends and the noise level of conversation started to rise again.

We made our way to the lounge.

'Where did you get that?' said Jill.

'Oh, I found it at home somewhere,' replied Jeanette. Her voice sounded unnatural – clipped and precise. It seemed to go with the dress. I remember thinking what a good actress she would make. She lifted the skirt of the dress slightly. 'It's silk velvet,' she said. 'Feel it – it's ever so soft.'

I took a little of the material between my fingers. It was very soft, but it also had a clamminess about it, and, close up, smelled musty, like an old attic. I reached up towards one of the cobwebs and began to brush it away. It crumbled, leaving a cloud of dust on the dress. Jeanette hardly seemed to notice.

Someone had changed the music to something that was more danceable. People were looking at each other as if they hoped someone else would start first.

Jeanette's eyes lit up. 'Dance!' she said, with enormous relish, and sashayed over to the floor where the carpet had been removed. People stared at her again, but she didn't care. We were all staring at her too. She was magnificent. Although the music had quite a fast beat she began to sway to it slowly, hampered by the skirt swirling slowly around her legs. She looked back and beckoned to us, her face full of life. I was tempted because I love to dance, but I wasn't sure if I could carry it off with the same amount of aplomb as she had.

While I was dithering, Jill pushed me forwards. 'Go on!' she hissed. 'We can't just leave her there!' I found myself propelled on to the dance floor.

We jogged and jiggered, feeling very ungraceful next to Jeanette, who was starting to move faster and faster. Suddenly she stopped and bent down to grasp the hem of her dress on the side seam. She posed one leg like she was about to do a tango and looked around us all with a wicked smile. Then, with a flourish, she pulled her hands apart sharply and ripped the skirt straight up the side practically to her hip.

There was a horrified intake of breath from everyone in the room.

As we were standing there stunned she burst out into raucous laughter. Then I was joining in too, followed a little uncertainly by the others. But I was caught up in her mood and found myself grasping my own hem and ripping hard. My efforts were greeted with whoops of encouragement. The skirt split after a few goes but not quite as far.

'Jeeze, Dianne!' breathed Jill in delighted horror.

Galvanised by the general sense of outrage we

were creating, Jeanette and I began to dance very fast, whirling around the dance floor like Catherine wheels. Then suddenly everyone was crowding on to the floor, whooping and gyrating with gay abandon. It seemed like the best party I'd ever been to.

I stumbled off in search of something to quench my thirst and bumped into Carla.

'Great party, Carla,' I puffed.

She took me to one side with an intrigued smile on her face. 'Where did you find her?'

'That's Jeanette Skelton – you know, the new girl?'

Carla had another good look at her on the dance floor. Jeanette's hair was starting to come down now. 'You mean quiet Jeanette who never says a word?'

I nodded.

'She certainly knows how to come out of her shell,' said Carla, with a raised eyebrow. 'Is she drunk?'

I couldn't imagine Jeanette hitting the bottle. 'No, I don't think so. She's just having a good time.'

Then someone came up behind me and Carla and put his arms around both of us. 'Hello, girls,' breathed a voice that sounded like its owner was trying to make it deeper than it naturally was. 'How about a cosy tête-à-tête?'

We both turned round and found ourselves looking into a spotty face with a beard that looked as if it was struggling to recover from a fight with a chicken plucker.

'Oh, hello, Guy,' said Carla, with distinct lack of interest. She wriggled free of his grasp. I did the same. 'Excuse me, I have to circulate. See you later, Di.' With that she was gone, leaving me alone with the biggest lech of the fifth year. Everyone knew he had pictures of topless girls in his locker.

Guy was grinning at me. 'Alone at last,' he said, and I hoped he was only joking.

'Guy,' I said. 'Let me give you a piece of advice. You are never going to be alone with anyone until you shave off that beard.'

He put his hand to his face and stroked the patchy clumps of hair. 'It takes time to get a good beard. In most achievements there is a period of struggle,' he added loftily. He made growing a beard sound like learning to play the Moonlight Sonata.

Someone moved past us and pushed us closer together. But immediately I could I pulled away from him again.

'Well, I'm sure it will be worth it when it's finished,' I said, and made to move away.

'If you won't have me, what about your dancing friend?' He indicated Jeanette, who was still prowling about the dance floor.

I didn't think it very likely somehow. He was a creep. 'Who knows?' I shrugged. Then I escaped to get a drink.

As I was coming back from the kitchen I heard him accosting some other poor girl. I walked past as inconspicuously as possible to hear her saying loudly, 'No thanks, I prefer a boy who has learned to shave.'

Jill and Sam were already cuddling up in a corner. I looked around for Ben, expecting him still to be on the dance floor with Jeanette. He wasn't, although she was still there – obviously she was a marathon-standard partyer.

'Care for a vol-au-vent?'

I turned around. Ben was standing with a plate heaped with crisps, vol-au-vents and cocktail sausages balanced on one hand like a waiter.

'I was just looking for you! I've been trying to fight off that creep Guy.'

'Fear not,' he said, 'I will protect you.' His hazel eyes twinkled. I giggled.

We went and sat on some floor cushions. My torn skirt flapped open and I did my best to cover my legs up. 'I might regret this in the morning,' I said, arranging the already fraying cloth.

It was nice and cosy eating party nibbles together, although I have to say that we had done this before and so it didn't have any special significance. I looked at Ben's broad shoulder and wondered if I dared to put my head on it, or at the very least snuggle up closer. But the bold mood that had come over me earlier was fast disappearing.

'Jeanette's getting to know Guy pretty well,' said Ben, indicating the dance floor. 'Is she flirting or is she trying to let him down gently?'

'She's probably flattered by the attention,' I mused. 'Wait until she finds out about the naughty pictures.'

The music changed to a slow, smoochy

number. I glanced quickly at Ben, wondering if I dared ask him for a dance, but I was sure he'd think I was joking.

'Good grief,' he said, looking at the dance floor.

I looked too. Jeanette was snuggled up in Guy's arms, apparently without complaint. They were swaying together gently like two trees in a breeze.

'That girl is full of surprises,' breathed Ben.

Just my luck, I thought miserably.

Guy moved his lips towards Jeanette's ear to whisper something. Then it all changed. I saw her expression turn angry and she suddenly pushed him away. When his arms didn't release her, she struggled harder. Guy loosened his hold a little and she leaned away from him. Drawing her arm back she brought it round to slap his face hard.

He let go of her immediately and she went for him again, raking her nails across his face and leaving deep red marks. She yelled something too, and he yelled back, but no one could hear what either of them was saying because of the music.

Then she pushed through the horrified people near by and headed for the door. The crowds parted for her as they had done a few hours ago when she made her entrance.

Ben and I were on our feet. Jill and Sam somehow found their way over to us, looking slightly dishevelled.

'We'd better go after her,' said Jill, her eyes

wide. She looked around at Sam and Ben. 'You two stay here. She's obviously had enough of blokes for the evening.' She grabbed my hand and pulled me after her.

'Us brutes will stay here then,' said Sam with a cheery wave.

We battled to the front door, which was standing open. Outside the air was cold. We stood in the front garden and looked around, waiting for our eyes to adjust to the dark.

'I can't see her anywhere,' said Jill.

'She can't have got far,' I said, stepping out into the road, tentatively looking up and down. I expected to see a fragile figure heading away from the house in a long dress, but there was no one.

Jill joined me. Suddenly she pointed. 'No, wait a minute – is that her?'

I peered harder into the dark. At the top of the road a figure was moving slowly. Too slowly. 'No,' I said, 'it's just an old woman.'

We had a look around in the front and back garden and still couldn't find her.

'That creep Guy,' I spluttered. 'What on earth did he say to her?'

'Something disgusting,' spat Jill. 'He ought to be locked up. We'd better go back in.'

The party seemed to be carrying on regardless. As we pushed through to find Ben and Sam a few smartasses said, 'Where's your wild friend? Has Cinderella run away?' We just ignored them.

I saw Guy first. He was standing with Ben and Sam, holding a paper napkin to his face.

'Honestly, she just went mad,' he was saying.

Ben and Sam looked at him with undisguised hostility, saying nothing.

'I didn't do a thing to her,' he protested. He removed the napkin and I saw the scratches had drawn blood. She must have really gone for him. 'She literally just went mad,' he said. The crowd around him remained sceptically silent. We moved to the kitchen.

'Maybe we should go round to her house to see if she's OK,' said Jill.

'It's a bit late to call on her,' said Sam, looking at his watch.

'And her mum won't let her have visitors,' I suddenly remembered.

'Hey, you guys,' said Ben, 'I'm afraid I have to be off.'

'Actually,' said Jill, looking at Sam, 'I don't think I feel like staying either.' She turned to me. 'Di, how about you?'

The party had lost all its sparkle for me, too, so we all said goodbye to Carla and headed out into the cold night. Jill, Sam and Ben walked me to my house.

'Maybe we should have gone to check on her,' I said uncertainly as I opened my front door.

'We'd only get her into trouble,' said Jill reassuringly. 'Perhaps she'll call on you tomorrow.'

They waved goodbye and I stepped into the welcoming warmth of home.

Jeanette didn't call on me the next day. Again I wondered whether I should go round there, but eventually I figured that if she hadn't got back safely everyone would know. And although I was worried about her I felt sure she wouldn't thank me for turning up uninvited, or worrying her parents about what might have happened to her at the party.

We didn't see her until school on Monday. Jill and I had managed to arrive together and I was having my usual battle with my locker door, virtually having to prise it open with a wooden ruler.

'There she is,' hissed Jill as she took the ruler from me to begin manipulating her own locker. 'Behind you.'

I turned around and she was almost right behind me. 'Jeanette!' I gasped, then burst into giggles. 'You shouldn't creep up on me like that.' Then I looked at her more closely. 'Are you OK?'

She nodded and managed a wan smile, but she looked terrible. She wasn't normally especially pale but today she looked almost ashen, her eyes big and dark. Her slight frame seemed so fragile she looked as if she might snap like a twig.

'Are you sure you're not ill?' I said gently.

She nodded vigorously and smiled again, that characteristically shy response. There was no trace of the self-confident creature we had seen on Saturday.

There was a shriek behind me as Jill tried to close her locker. She came to join us, sucking her fingers. 'Somone's going to lose some limbs one day in those things,' she snorted, giving me back the ruler. She looked at Jeanette. 'Were you OK on Saturday?'

'Yes,' said Jeanette in a small voice. The bell went and we started to amble along to assembly. Soon we were caught in a tide of people.

'Sam and Ben nearly hit Guy,' Jill said with vehemence.

Jeanette looked into the distance and allowed herself to be borne away in the crowd. Jill started to try to catch up with her but an instinct made me put a hand on her arm to stop her.

'Leave her,' I said. 'She wants to be on her own.'

Jill caught sight of Guy, fortunately safely out of reach. 'Look who's over there.' She snarled an expletive. 'What did he try to do to her to make her behave like that?'

THREE

That Wednesday I got home from school to find my brother Mark leaping around in delight because he'd passed his driving test.

'Great!' I said. 'Now you can pick me up from parties instead of Mum or Dad and I can stay out later!'

'Oh no you don't, young lady,' called Mum's voice from the kitchen. 'Parental Taxis Inc still has the monopoly in this house.' She came bustling through to the dining room. 'But you can take the car down to the shops to get me some milk,' she said, taking a note out of her purse and handing it to him.

Mark was still too excited by the novelty to consider such a thing a chore. And like most boys he also wanted to show off to his younger sister. 'Come on, Di, I'll take you for a spin,' he said, grabbing my hand and pulling me out.

'All right, I'm coming,' I mumbled. 'Just let me get my crash helmet.'

'Drive carefully,' called Mum's voice as we pushed the front door shut.

We got into the car and put our seatbelts on.

Mark put the key in the ignition. 'You know,'

he said, with what I thought was inappropriate cheeriness, 'this is the first time I've driven someone who knows less than I do.' He started the car and the engine roared with a flourish.

'Right, you plonker,' I said, 'I'm getting out.'

But before I could undo my seat belt he started to roll the car forward. I sat back and relaxed instead.

I have to say that although Mark, like all brothers, is a bit of an idiot at times and a pain in the backside at others, he is actually too sensible to take risks. Not many people, for example, pass their test first time. What happened next could not possibly have been his fault.

He took the car slowly to the edge of the drive, and stopped and looked both ways before pulling out. I looked too and I swear there was nobody there.

He began to ease the car over the kerb and into the road. One minute he was a picture of calmness and the next – I heard him take a deep breath very sharply. His eyes had darted up to the mirror.

'What the hell's that?' He braked and put one hand up to adjust the mirror.

I don't know what happened next. He insisted later that he hadn't hit the wrong pedal, that the car just surged forward by itself. Suddenly we were careering towards the other side of the road at a terrifying speed. I screamed.

Mark was shouting, his foot pumping on the brake pedal. He took hold of the steering wheel and wrenched it over to the left, and the car seemed to swivel alarmingly. I screamed again and covered my eyes. Mark swore and I could hear him twisting the wheel the other way.

Then there was a horrible-sounding bump and we seemed to run over something. Mark swore again and the car finally came to a stop.

I leaned forward in my seat like an airline passenger in crash position, shaking and breathing hard.

'You OK?' Mark gasped.

'Yeah.' I felt close to tears, but tried not to give in to them.

'I hit something,' he said, without raising his head. 'I don't want to look.'

'I don't want to either,' I said, looking at the floor and keeping a hold on the wobble in my voice.

'Please,' he said. 'You look.' He tilted his head so that he was looking at me.

I told myself it was just going to be a large piece of wood or the spare tyre, and then I straightened up to look out of the windscreen.

There was nothing.

Of course. It was behind us. I fumbled with the latch and stumbled out on to the road. A bloodied shape was heaving itself painfully towards the pavement, leaving behind it a sticky dark trail. As I approached I began to hear a tiny whimper coming from it.

I shrieked, 'Mark, get out, it's Bubbles!' I ran over to him, but the dog had made it to the pavement and was pulling himself over the ornamental front-garden wall.

'Bubbles!' I sobbed. 'Bubbles, stay!' I was so afraid he would injure himself more if he moved. But the heroic animal made it over the wall. I prayed that this was a sign that he would be all right. My stomach turned somersaults when I heard him let out a low growl.

A figure was standing in the drive, in front of the garage. For a moment I was transfixed. Then I realised it was Jeanette, standing stiff like a manikin, staring ahead in a way that freaked me out even more.

'I came to apologise,' she said calmly. It was as if she hadn't seen what had happened, but I put it down to shock. We were all pretty shaken.

Bubbles growled softly again. Mark had knelt down beside him, but was immediately up on his feet and in through the front door, shouting, 'Mum! Call the vet!'

I knelt down. I wanted to touch Bubbles or cradle his head but I didn't dare in case I made him worse. All I could do was talk to him quietly, which I did through sobs. There was so much blood. He had left a thick smear of it over the garden wall. 'It's OK, Bubbles,' I said softly. Mum and Mark had come to the door. Mark was practically in tears. I could hear him saying, 'Honestly, I just saw something in the mirror, then the car went out of control.' Mum put an arm around him and he didn't resist.

Jeanette stepped closer and knelt down. 'Would it be better if I came back some other time?' Her voice was very quiet but it jerked a response from Bubbles. He managed to raise his

29

muzzle and put his ears flat against his bloodied head. Another growl came from somewhere inside him, stronger than the last time, and now accompanied by red froth. I could see his body shrinking from her. He continued to growl at Jeanette until she stood up and left.

FOUR

Dad, Mark and I put Bubbles' favourite blanket over the body and Mum went to collect the
car from the other side of the road. We watched
as she drove it round the block. Then she called
to Mark to drive it into the garage. He was
reluctant, but she insisted, saying he'd never get
behind the wheel again otherwise. Looking pale
and shaken, he piloted the car into the garage
perfectly.

They got out and she walked round to the
driver's seat, giving him another hug as she
moved past him. He squirmed out of her
embrace. 'You're OK, kiddo,' she said, giving his
shoulder a push. 'Stay there, everybody.'

Then she reversed the car out again, drove a
little way down the road and halted. 'Mark, come
and get in again and you can drive Di into the
garage this time.'

I made as if to refuse, but she was adamant. I
knew we would be there all night if that's how
long it took. Mark took the driver's seat, I got in
the passenger side and Mum got in the back. She

31

kept the atmosphere in the car calm and Mark executed another perfect garage entry.

No one could face eating much that night. We tried to hide what had happened from Charlie, but he's a sensitive kid and knew something was wrong. He cried and refused to eat.

Dad and Mark dug a grave in the front garden and put Bubbles in, and only then did we let Charlie see. He helped to fill in the hole.

'Come on, now,' said Dad as we stood there in the chilly night. 'We'd better go inside. I'm phoning the garage about that car first thing tomorrow.'

My window looks out on to the front of the house. Before I went to sleep I spent a long time staring out at the grave, which was almost invisible in the dark. What seemed most shocking was the speed with which it had all happened, how quickly a celebration had turned to a tragedy. For the first time I thought about how vulnerable we are. That could just as easily have been Charlie who got hit, or even Jeanette – who must have arrived while it was happening. In fact she must have seen it. Maybe, when I was feeling more together, I would ask her if she saw anything that could have caused it. I remembered her strange expression as we were in the drive. She'd been so shocked.

Finally I got into bed and put out the light. I didn't feel tired, but I had school the next day and had to get some sleep. I lay there awake for what seemed ages, and then kept waking up feeling like I hadn't been asleep at all. I must have been drifting in and out of dreams, as if I were in the middle of a scene that was really happening in the room and would then be interrupted. I kept seeing Jeanette, standing stiffly in front of the garage door with her eyes staring into the distance in a way that was extremely scary. I would see it and the panic would build up in me and I would wake, looking around half expecting to see a ghost.

I would settle back into the pillows again and presently be seeing either that image of Jeanette or the strange reflection I saw in the shop window during the storm the previous Saturday. In my confused mind the two became interchangeable. In the tumble of images my brain kept replaying to me I started to see Mark clinging on to Mum and saying he'd seen a figure in the mirror, which had made him swerve. Then I would be back to seeing Jeanette or the shop window. The only thing I saw of Bubbles was him growling at Jeanette.

I woke up early the next morning and remembered all this, which is unusual as I rarely recall my dreams. I often remember if I've dreamed about someone, though, and sometimes it colours the way I think of them, but only for a short time. I don't think I'd ever had such spooky dreams and they made me start to see Jeanette in a different way. I suddenly remembered how she was prone to these mood changes – in fact I'd never seen anyone able to go to such extremes. Was there something wrong with her? That's when I first started to wonder.

I washed and dressed and went down to breakfast. Everyone was trying to act as if nothing had happened, and I told myself not to let my imagination run away with me.

I got into school and had my usual locker fight before assembly. Jill was late, so I wasn't able to tell her very much before we had to be quiet and pay attention, or rather I didn't feel like blabbing about all that had happened where everyone else could hear. Jeanette came in late, too, looking pale again. I tentatively waved to her as she joined the end of a row. Somehow I felt that I might upset her if I wasn't very careful.

Fortunately Jill and I had the first lesson free. Jeanette had Latin. I always thanked my lucky stars that my parents never made me learn a dead language.

Jill, Ben and I took one of our long walks to the school library, and I told them all about the night before. I mentioned Jeanette coming round and seeing it all, but none of my wilder ideas about whether she was entirely *compos mentis*. I told them about the burial, and Mark and me having to get our nerves back in the car. It was that that finally had me in tears. They mopped me up, and Ben gave me a brotherly hug.

We met Jeanette on the way to history, and she was looking even more drained. We had just got to the door of the classroom when she swayed as though she were drunk, then fell heavily forwards. Ben reached for her and managed to stop her crashing to the ground.

'Quick, somebody get a teacher!' I yelled.

Some people came up to have a closer look, and some came out of the classroom to see what was going on.

Jill threw down her books. 'Don't just stand there!' she shouted at them, pushing through into the classroom.

Fortunately Mrs Colney, the history teacher, had heard the commotion and swept in. 'Give her some air,' she said coolly. 'Jill, go to the office and tell them what's happened.' Jeanette's eyes were fluttering open again and she was looking round, bewildered.

Jill was away immediately.

'Right, Dianne and Ben, you stay here. The rest of you go to your desks.' The general level of excitement raised in pitch. 'And stay quiet,' Mrs Colney called.

Jill came back with the school nurse, who had brought a wheelchair. The nurse helped Jeanette to her feet. She was deathly white and looked like she would collapse again any minute.

'Is she going to be all right?' I asked the nurse quietly while she settled Jeanette, protesting, into a chair.

She nodded. 'She's started to get bad period pains, that's all. We telephoned her mother and that's what she told us. She's coming to collect her. Nothing to worry about. You can all get back to your class now.'

With that they wheeled her away. I'd never seen anyone look so ill from such 'natural' causes before, and I suspected something far worse was wrong.

FIVE

I was rather surprised to see Jeanette back in school on Friday and exuding health. But then she did seem to be turning into a creature of curious extremes – either a fragile, fainting ghost or a wild, unstable dynamo.

Ben had approached me as I was wrestling my locker open. The look on his face suggested he wanted to talk about something serious. Immediately my heart gave a flutter of excitement and my brain sternly told me to be sensible. But it was coming up to Valentine's Day and I was rather more romantically aware than usual.

He leaned closer so that we could talk quietly in the general morning hubbub. 'I don't know if it's too soon to mention this but – ' He seemed to feel awkward and looked down.

'Come on, Ben, out with it,' I said, and then was astonished at my boldness. Some of Jeanette's super-confidence must have been rubbing off on me.

He smiled and started again. 'Well, my aunt's got some Labrador puppies she wants to find good homes for, if you wanted one. But I suppose you may not want to yet, or you may not want one the same, or . . .' He trailed off. 'It was just a suggestion.'

I was quite taken aback. And I also felt a pang of disappointment – not only, I am ashamed to say, because I had got my hopes up about Valentine's Day, but also because thinking about Bubbles made me remember my new-found fear of the general fragility of life.

'OK, dumb idea,' said Ben.

'No, no,' I countered hastily. 'It's a lovely idea. But I think it is too soon. Thanks, though.' Then I felt awkward and couldn't think of anything else to say.

'Hi, Ben! Hi, Di!'

Startled out of our tête-à-tête we both looked up to see Jeanette bounding past energetically, glossy blue-black hair streaming behind her like in a commercial for expensive shampoo.

'Jeanette!' I exclaimed, following her to her locker. 'How are you feeling?'

She was rummaging in her locker. 'Oh, I'm fine now.' She swung the locker door shut and heaved her rucksack on to her shoulder. 'The list for the swimathon team is on the sports board today. Coming to look?'

'Oh yeah! I forgot,' said Ben.

We followed her to the sports notice-board at the end of the cloakroom. People were crowded around it about three deep, but Jeanette pushed through.

'You, me and Jill are in!' she exclaimed happily, and then came back out again.

'When are the practices?' Ben asked.

'Tuesdays and Thursdays,' she replied.

'Rather you than me,' I muttered.

A voice rang out across the cloakroom. 'Jeanette? Can I have a word?'

Jeanette looked round. The form teacher, Miss Warburton, was beckoning in our direction.

'Wonder what I've done? See you in a mo,' said Jeanette.

We were on our way into assembly when she reappeared.

'So, was it a crime to faint in class yesterday?' said Jill, who had joined us.

Jeanette pulled a face. 'I've got to read the lesson.' She had a Bible in her hand. 'It's our form's turn and she "thought I might like to do it because I'm the new girl".' The disgust in her voice was barely disguised.

Ben gave her a friendly pat on the back. 'Bad luck.'

We filed into the assembly hall and shuffled along the pew-like rows to our seats. As Jeanette sat down next to me she leaned over and said in a low voice, 'By the way, I'm so sorry about your dog.'

I gave her a quick smile. 'Thanks.'

Then, as we all had to stand up for the start of assembly she stayed sitting down and leaned forward. From her copious rucksack she took a large, old-looking hand mirror.

I was distracted from seeing what she did next by Jill nudging me to point out the music teacher's odd socks – one brown and one red.

'That proves he's colour blind,' she hissed.

'Not necessarily. It might be a fashion state-ment,' I countered.

We all sat down for the headmistress to give her daily address. Jeanette still had the mirror, and was absorbed in looking into it. Not in a vain sort of way; she wasn't adjusting her hair or the minimal amount of make-up she was wearing. It was more like a state of deep fascination. She tilted the mirror gently and the light coming in through the high windows of the assembly hall was reflected on the ceiling in a brilliant white pool. She didn't look around at the effect at all, but simply carried on drinking in the image in the mirror.

'Today's lesson will be read by Jeanette Skel-ton.' The headmistress looked around, expecting to see someone rise to their feet.

Jeanette hadn't heard. She must have been deeply absorbed in her own thoughts, because even if I'm paying attention when a teacher calls my name I always find myself startled by it. I nudged her as the headmistress called her name again. Jeanette heard this time, stuffed the mirror back in her bag and stood up. Then, agitated, she sat down again to pick up the Bible and fumbled, dropping it. I leaned down to help her, hoping to calm her down. She got to her feet again and scrambled past the rest of the row and round the side of the hall to the steps of the stage.

Poor thing, I thought. She's really nervous. Jeanette made her way to the lectern and started to fumble with the pages of the Bible.

'Maybe she'll faint again,' sneered a voice

behind me. Furious, I turned around to see Carla grinning with her cronies. Sometimes she was such a cow.

After a little more fumbling, Jeanette began to read. 'Blessed are they that mourn: for they shall be comforted,' she read tonelessly. 'Blessed are the meek: for they shall inherit the earth.'

My mind was starting to drift when she paused, and then closed the book. She looked up and around, taking her time to note her surroundings. Suddenly she didn't seem to be nervous any more.

A strange look came over her face. It was like a smile, but one that lit up her eyes as if a spotlight had been turned on her, or as if the roving pool of light from her mirror had settled on her.

The assembled school started to make an uncomfortable shifting sound. She stood there and looked slowly around us all. Snatches of conversation began to be exchanged in whispers. Most people standing on a stage alone would have crumbled under that sort of attention but she retained her poise. Even the staff seemed temporarily paralysed.

'Let's put this in more modern terms. If life has dealt you some cruel blows, just let yourself be overwhelmed by them. If you creep around quietly and never fight back you'll be very successful.' An ironic smile crossed Jeanette's face and a ripple of quiet laughter went through the audience.

'Now think about that. Does that sound like

good advice? Does it sound plausible? Would any of you believe it? Does any area of life bear out the theory that if you give up when faced with difficulty you will be rewarded?' Another ripple of laughter from the pupils, but the staff were looking distinctly wary.

'No, of course not. It's preposterous. Now – ' She picked the Bible up and riffled through the pages towards the front. There was no trace of fumbling this time.

'This is more like it,' she said with satisfaction. '"And thine eye shall not pity; but life shall go for life, eye for eye, tooth for tooth . . . " There are old farts who would try to convince us that "the meek shall inherit the earth". But we know different. We know we have to seize our chances while we can. Particularly if we have youth on our side.' A murmur of approval rumbled through the audience. The staff seemed to have decided to go with the flow.

'When we're knocked down we have to get back up again. We can lick our wounds for a while but then we have to get up and carry on fighting. Life is for taking hold of with both hands. It is for squeezing as hard as possible. If we don't take what we can someone else will.' The audience murmured agreement again, more loudly, but hushed the moment Jeanette started to speak.

'We may be told that because we're young we shouldn't be in a hurry, shouldn't try to do things too fast. We're told we've got all the time in the world.'

She fixed the audience with an intense stare,

and then dropped her voice to a whisper. 'We haven't.'

The school's anticipation was tangible, like a concert audience waiting for the final crashing notes of a symphony. Jeanette was playing them like a skilful conductor. She waited just long enough before repeating, with just enough emphasis, 'We haven't.' Then she picked up the Bible, stepped back from the lectern and left the stage.

The school started to clap. There were a few delighted whoops but they quickly subsided into politely decorous applause, as if, after all, nobody really knew whether to be impressed or censorious. Personally, I would have given her a standing ovation; what she had said really struck a chord in me after what had happened with Bubbles and all the things it had made me think about. She had said exactly what I needed to hear – it was as if she had intuitively guessed all the things I needed reassurance about, although she had chosen an overdramatic way of going about it. I'd never before come across anyone with such a capacity to do the truly unexpected.

When the headmistress came back on to the stage her mouth was set in a prim disapproving line. 'Thank you, Jeanette, for that. Come and see me afterwards.'

Typical teacher, I thought. She was an embodiment of the attitude Jeanette had been talking about.

'Uh-oh, she's going to be in big trouble,' whispered Jill.

'It was rather over the top,' said Ben.

The headmistress called out for quiet as the whispers spread around the hall. I decided I would make sure I thanked Jeanette afterwards. However odd her outburst had been she'd done a gutsy thing and deserved to be acknowledged. She joined us as we filed out. People went quiet as we all went past them, their conversation becoming scandalised whispers. I'd never realised before how shallow most people's stance of rebellion is. Or did they just like to anticipate the trouble Jeanette was going to be in? I distinctly remember we came up behind a first-year, a good-looking blonde kid called Charlotte Watling. She can't have known we were there because she was saying in quite a loud voice, 'Those fifth-formers are just all on drugs. They're so OTT.' Jeanette's face turned to thunder. I thought she might be about to hit the girl.

Later at break I asked her what the headmistress had said to her, and she just shrugged and said, 'The usual.'

'Well, I thought what you did was great,' I said, feeling rather inadequate in my choice of words. Jeanette blushed and said dismissively, 'I don't really remember much of it.' And then Ben appeared and the subject changed to the swimathon.

Jeanette may not have remembered much of what she said, but I did. The more I thought about it the more disturbing I found it. The very fact that she had had the guts to do it was a source of wonder in itself. I particularly remembered her saying, 'These people tell you we have all the time in the world. We haven't.' And her fury later when she heard Charlotte Watling sneer – surely that was more than just an over-sensitive ego? Was there something wrong with her? 'We must seize life with both hands and squeeze it dry . . .' When I remember those words now they chill me to the bone. And her heartfelt, whispered: 'We haven't.' In a way she was telling us what was going on, what was eating away at her. And we had all just sat there and laughed and applauded politely, thinking she was giving rousing speeches for the hell of it.

SIX

I'd arranged to meet Jill in the coffee shop on Saturday. It seemed like ages since we'd had a good natter. Of course, the first thing she said once we were at a table and huddling over our steaming mugs of cappuccino was: 'Are you sending a valentine card to Ben?' I went red and giggled. 'Oh, go on,' cooed my shameless friend. 'You must.'

I started to eat the froth of my cappuccino with a spoon. 'Well, I wondered whether to, but – oh, I don't know . . .' I took refuge in a slurp of cocoa-speckled foam.

'Now let's get this straight,' said Jill in a businesslike manner. 'You have got to do some thinking about what you want. No – ' she said, putting her hand up as I started to interrupt. 'You're nuts about him. You know you are. If he sent you a valentine card what would you do? You'd be in seventh heaven. Well, you don't know if he's going to send you one, so if you want a date with him you've got to do some of the running. And this is the perfect time.'

I sighed. 'You might be right . . . but I always thought that guys thought sending valentines was rather immature. Whenever you hear them talk about having got cards they're always laughing about it. It's a big joke to them.'

'Yeah, that might be a problem. OK, you don't have to make it a valentine thing. But I do think you ought to do something soon. He might not hang on for ever.'

I smiled ruefully. 'I doubt that he's hanging on at all, at least not for me.' Jill raised an eyebrow. I went on. 'It may be my imagination but I think he'd like to go out with Jeanette. He's been quite protective about her since that episode with Guy at Carla's party.'

'No!' she said scornfully.

I stirred my now frothless drink. 'Well, I have been keeping an eye on him. Or maybe he just does his big-brother act with her as well.'

'Hmm . . . you do have a point.' She looked at me mischievously. 'Then you'd better get in first!'

I shook my head. 'No,' I said emphatically. 'I'm not very good at coping with rejection, and I don't want to get better at it by practising on Ben. It would be too awful. Period.' I signalled to the waitress as she went by and ordered some more coffees, and took advantage of the natural break to steer the subject away from Ben. Anything but get more nagging about that. Of course, the other obvious thing to talk about was Jeanette. 'What do you think of Jeanette?'

'What do you mean?' Jill drained the last of her cup.

'Well . . . I've got a hunch about her . . .'

Jill's eyes widened. She leaned forward on her elbows. 'What sort of hunch? Do tell.'

Actually I wasn't sure where to start. I realised that my intuitions about her were no more than that; I couldn't think of many concrete examples of odd behaviour that would convince a third party. 'She seems to change so much.' Jill frowned so I elaborated. 'One minute she's shy and very quiet, the next she's clowning around or delivering impulsive speeches and horrifying the staff.'

Jill waved her hand dismissively, narrowly missing the waitress who had come back with our second coffees. 'She's just highly strung,' she said. 'Quite extraordinarily highly strung, I admit, but no more than that.'

'But what about the party? That dress and everything, and the way she went wild?'

'Oh, that's just because she'd dressed up in a vampish costume. Don't you feel different in glamorous clothes as well?'

'No, I didn't mean the dancing. I meant later, with Guy. She really had a go at him.'

Jill's mouth became an uncompromising line. 'He's a creep and he deserved it. Serves him right for picking on the wrong kind of girl.'

I bit my lip. 'Yeah, I suppose so. But she wouldn't talk about it afterwards at all.'

Jill drew a heart shape in the foam of her drink. 'She's probably just very sensitive,' she said slowly. 'Not everyone feels they can talk to people about things that have upset them and, don't forget, she doesn't know any of us that well yet.'

'You're right. I suppose she isn't that odd after all. I just started wondering about whether she was ill or something when she collapsed the other day.'

'Yes, that is a bit unusual. But she probably only fainted. Maybe she hadn't done her history homework. I've often been tempted to try a fainting fit to get out of maths.' She giggled and then her eyes widened as she stared past me to the door.

'What's the matter?' I said.

'Talk of the devil,' she muttered.

I turned around. Jeanette had just walked in through the door and was heading for the bread counter. Jill put her fingers between her teeth and managed an impressive wolf whistle. About half a dozen people seemed to turn around, and fortunately one of them was Jeanette or the other customers would have had to endure the ear-piercing sound again. She came over and turned a chair round so that the back faced her, then sat down straddling the seat. It's a position that can look really cool if you have the confidence to carry it off. She had.

'I caught up with you at last,' she said with a big smile. 'My mum sent me in here to get some bread. So,' she said, leaning forward, 'what's the gossip?'

'Uh-uh,' said Jill shaking her head. 'You first. Who are you sending a valentine card to?'

Jeanette looked nonplussed. 'Why? Have I got one sticking out of my pocket?' Then she laughed. 'Actually, yes I did have one idea.' She paused. 'I thought of sending one to our poor old form teacher. What do you think?'

I tried to imagine Miss Warburton, a confirmed spinster if ever there was one, discovering a communication of a suspectedly romantic nature in her desk, and found the idea irresistible.

'Hey, yeah!' said Jill, eyes glittering. 'A joke one or a serious-looking one?'

'Oh, a serious-looking one of course,' I said immediately. 'Valentine's Day is all a big joke anyway.'

'I suppose so,' agreed Jill. 'And anyway, a card has got to let you dream a little.'

I looked at my watch and realised I was supposed to be getting home. I hurriedly waved at the waitress for the bill. 'I've got to be going,' I said, 'but the corner shop has got a brilliant selection of slushy cards that will probably do nicely. I'll get one on the way home.'

Jeanette jumped up. 'Yeah, that sounds great. We can stick it in her desk on Monday.' She looked round. 'Look, I wanted to invite you guys over but my mum still won't let me.' She grimaced. 'I think she doesn't want me to have a social life. But maybe in the next few weeks . . .'

'Don't worry about it,' I smiled. 'There's no rush.'

Jeanette grinned, relieved. 'Anyway,' she said

briskly as the bill arrived and Jill and I settled up, 'I'd better be off to join the bread queue.'

Of course she's perfectly normal, I was telling myself as I left the café. When it comes down to it she's just a bit of a hell-raiser.

SEVEN

On my way home on Saturday I'd got the perfect
card, the kind that would be laughed at by
anyone of our age but probably thought of as
quite pleasant by Miss Warburton. When I
showed it to Jeanette and Jill on Monday they
gave out little squeals of delight, and we hurriedly
composed a cryptic message. Jeanette wrote it,
disguising her handwriting.

It was innocent at the time, but when I look
back on it I cringe as I remember what it led to –
and how my insistence on using a 'serious' card
made matters ten times worse. And it was I who
slipped the card into Miss Warburton's desk just
moments before she sailed in through the classroom door to take registration. I could almost
feel Jeanette's and Jill's excitement as any
moment we expected her to open the desk and
find the pale pink envelope – but of course she
didn't.

For the rest of the day we were speculating on
whether she had opened it yet, and tried to watch
her surreptitiously for signs that she had – an
unusual glitter to the eyes or a pink flush across
the cheeks. By the time history came round, the

first period of the afternoon, we hadn't detected anything obvious.

Mrs Colney was giving back essays that we'd written as part of a project on the early part of the twentieth century. The subject had been an aspect of everyday life at that time, and we also had to bring in an everyday object or find a picture of something relevant. I had chosen the War Poets, and had brought in a picture of Wilfred Owen.

Mrs Colney came to Jeanette's essay. 'Ah yes,' she said, 'the flu epidemic of 1918 . . . Interesting that you chose to do it in the first person, even though I hadn't asked you to. Is that how you used to do them at your last school?'

Jeanette shook her head.

'It just occurred to you on the spur of the moment, then?'

Jeanette nodded.

'Well, it was very effective. An interesting choice of topic, very vividly written and highly detailed. I almost felt I was there. Where did you get all your information? Do you have a book on the flu epidemic at home?'

'My great-grandmother died in it,' said Jeanette simply.

Mrs Colney looked a little taken aback, but recovered her composure enough to make an educational point. 'Well, there you are, everybody: history brought to life again.' Then she addressed Jeanette, holding out the essay for her to collect. 'Well done. But don't write all your essays as if they were diaries.' She gave a friendly smile.

Jeanette's seat was next to mine, and when she came back I looked at the essay. She had not used her normal handwriting but a copperplate script, uncannily like the sort of writing that my grandparents were still being taught when they went to school. But I didn't have a chance to remark on it, as Mrs Colney was asking us to display and talk about the objects or pictures we'd brought in.

I read out one of Wilfred Owen's poems to go with my picture. Jill had managed to unearth a gasmask and tried to tie it in with the passage I had chosen but was scornfully shouted down by the boys in the class, who told her that it was actually from World War II.

One of the guys had brought in a fragment of china – all that remained of some ancient tea service. He held up the little piece of porcelain between finger and thumb and then couldn't think of what to say about it, so we all burst out laughing. At this he went rather pink, which made him look as if he was about to explain that he had broken it, so we all laughed even more.

Most people had brought pictures, though, and it began to get a bit boring hearing the same old stuff about kings, queens and prime ministers.

Jeanette, in her usual style, had managed to do something completely different. She brought out the hand mirror I had seen her with a few days earlier. 'This,' she said, 'belonged to my great-grandmother.'

There was a general sound of 'oohh'. All the

other objects belonged to dead people, but this one seemed more personal. We crowded around Jeanette to try to have a look in it, but Mrs Colney told us to sit down. I was fascinated to see my reflection in a mirror that had once reflected the face of a woman who had now been dead for almost 80 years. It seemed to form an eerily direct link with her.

Or maybe that's my imagination embroidering things after the event.

After a while Mrs Colney looked at her watch. 'Well,' she said, 'it's nearly time for the bell. It's been very interesting seeing what you've all brought. I don't know if you're aware that the school is having an open day in a couple of weeks, but I'd like to make a display out of the best objects we've seen today.' She read out a few names. Jill's gas mask was wanted, and my picture, and Jeanette's mirror.

Jill and I got up to take our items to Mrs Colney's desk, but Jeanette stayed where she was. I nudged her and indicated to her to follow me, but she shook her head firmly and clasped the mirror's handle in both hands.

'No,' she said in a low voice.

'What's the matter, Jeanette?' said the teacher.

'It's not going on display,' she replied.

'Is that because your parents will object?' asked Mrs Colney kindly. She got up and went to stand in front of Jeanette's desk.

'No.'

'Then why? We'll be very careful with it. I will personally see that no harm comes to it. I can see why you would be worried about it. It is a very unusual mirror.' She reached forward as if to try and have a closer look at it, but Jeanette snatched it away.

'I said no!'

Mrs Colney saw she was beaten and backed away. 'Any more behaviour like that and you'll be here in detention after school,' she said quietly, looking extremely rattled.

Then the bell went. Jeanette got hurriedly to her feet and thrust the mirror into her rucksack, then her books. She ignored everyone else around her and was first out of the door.

'I think I'm beginning to see what you mean about Jeanette being so odd,' murmured Jill to me as we gathered up our books and joined the crush.

EIGHT

Jeanette was very quiet in the next lesson, and wasn't in biology, the last one that afternoon.

Jill, Ben and I arranged the seats on the back bench so that Jeanette's absence didn't look too obvious.

'I don't think she's skipped a lesson before,' Ben said.

'She must be finding her feet,' said Jill, her eyes twinkling in anticipation of mischief. 'Maybe we've only just started finding out what she's really like.'

'I suppose we'll never know what Miss Warburton made of her valentine,' I mused.

'We should have sent one with a badge,' said Jill.

'She probably wouldn't have worn it,' I replied. 'She can't be that desperate.'

'No, probably not.'

Later, I was on the bus going home and off in a dream world. Someone came to sit in the seat next to me, so I moved my bag without really looking at who it was.

Then a familiar voice said, 'You've got to get off with me at the next stop.'

I looked round, startled. 'Jeanette! What happened to you this afternoon?'

'I had a few things to arrange,' she replied nonchalantly. No sooner had she sat down than she got up again to ring the bell. 'Come on.'

I got up too. 'But, Jeanette, this is the middle of the high street. What's going on?'

The bus drew to a halt, the doors folded back and Jeanette got off. She beckoned me impatiently.

I followed, intrigued. 'Where are we going?' I almost had to run to keep up with her.

'You'll see,' she replied, eyes dancing with excitement. Her mood was infectious and I allowed myself to be pulled along by it.

We had reached the coffee shop. 'Have you got a caffeine craving?' I said as she dragged me in.

We ordered cappuccinos and Jeanette picked out a tiny table behind a column. She leaned forward conspiratorially. 'Look over there,' she whispered, inclining her head. 'Not too obviously.'

I tilted my head in what I hoped was a casual way but probably telegraphed to everyone what I was doing. Seated to our left, just visible around the column, was Miss Warburton.

I looked back at Jeanette immediately.

'She shouldn't be able to see us here,' she said reassuringly.

Emboldened, I looked again. Miss Warburton was at a table by herself, and she appeared to be rather agitated. She kept taking tiny sips at a cup of hot chocolate and then glancing around nervously.

I turned back to Jeanette. 'She's waiting for someone!' I hissed incredulously.

Jeanette had a quick peep around the column before hunching back over the table. 'I put a note in her desk, after you put the card in.' She spoke quickly in her excitement. 'I told her to be at the café at four, and to wear a pink carnation!' She burst into a fit of giggles.

I had to look around the pillar again. Miss Warburton was indeed sporting a large, pale pink carnation in her buttonhole. She looked at her watch and then took another sip of chocolate.

'She should be drinking something a bit stronger than Ovaltine,' snickered Jeanette. 'Imagine you were going on a blind date – would you have a quick snifter of Horlicks to set you up?'

I shook my head.

'And anyway, it'll make her moustache bigger.' She gave a high, nervous giggle.

I looked at my watch. It said five past four. I looked round at Miss Warburton again. She was growing even more agitated. It was strange to see a teacher in a position where she couldn't control what was going on. I began to feel a bit uncomfortable about spying on her.

She consulted her watch twice in the short time that I was looking and began to fiddle with the carnation in her buttonhole. It was tantamount to wearing a badge. I recalled what I'd been saying to Jill earlier and realised Miss Warburton might well be desperate. How horrible to be her age and lonely.

'Jeanette,' I said, 'is anybody coming to meet her? I mean, what are we doing here?'

Jeanette gave a crafty smile.

I carried on, a little uncertainly. 'We're not just going to sit here and see how long she waits, are we?'

Jeanette flagged down a passing waitress. 'No, of course not,' she said quickly as she paid her bill. 'She'll have run out of Ovaltine in a minute and we don't want her to drift off. Come on.' She was on her feet immediately.

I paid and followed her out of the café. Jeanette took a last look to check Miss Warburton was still carrying on her vigil and then grabbed my arm and steered me into the phone box outside the café.

It was a bit of a squeeze, particularly when Jeanette reached into her pocket for something. She brought out a book of matches from the café. I watched, bemused, as she dialled the number. She was hopping up and down with excitement now, practically hyperactive. I tried to let myself be carried along by it but I had a few doubts about what she might be up to. But it was too late to back out now.

'Hello?' said Jeanette, and leaned across to look into the café. The person who had answered the phone was clearly visible through the front window. Jeanette deepened her voice. 'Do you have a Miss Warburton in your establishment? I believe she is wearing a pink flower in her buttonhole.'

I thought the deepened voice was going rather over the top, but the café manager looked around her customers. Miss Warburton had been scanning the door for anyone coming in and had been instantly put on the alert when the phone rang. She responded immediately when the manager held out the receiver and beckoned her over. Jeanette gave a huge grin like some man-eating animal.

Miss Warburton's face was alive with expectation and she knocked over her nearly empty cup in her haste to get to the phone. She didn't even stop to pick it up, which was astonishing because she is usually rather a fussy person. I began to have a very bad feeling about being involved in this.

I watched her take the handset and I heard her cautious 'H-hello'. Then Jeanette burst into a demented shrieking laugh that was hideously shrill in the confined space. I saw Miss Warburton's face register first incomprehension and then bitter hurt and humiliation, and I looked away quickly. Jeanette was still laughing and leaned over so that she got the best view possible. I gladly moved out of her way. I tried to yell at her to stop but she seemed unable to hear me. So I pushed past her and out of the phone box and ran away as fast as I could.

NINE

I didn't go straight home. I went for a walk and ended up at the school playing fields, which, as I hoped they might be, were empty. I couldn't face coming into contact with anyone I knew. I walked for a long time in the cold, and it began to rain but I just carried on. I felt I deserved to be wet and cold. In fact I deserved a lot more.

How could I have become involved in that? I was more ashamed than I have ever been in my entire life. I know everyone thinks teachers are fair game for the odd prank – I'd be the first to agree. But that was well out of order. I kept seeing the expression on that poor woman's face, first when she was called to the phone and then when Jeanette started laughing.

How could Jeanette have done a thing like that? It was like the kind of cruelty a first-year might inflict on someone, but not the way some-body of our age would behave. It wasn't just immature, it was downright wicked, inhuman.

I winced as I remembered choosing a card that wouldn't look like it was a joke, and how I put it in Miss Warburton's desk. But that was perfectly innocent fun – the kind of prank you do and then never hear anything else about. Miss Warburton probably wouldn't be able to trace Jeanette and myself as the culprits, but that didn't make me feel any better.

Jill and I had sometimes wondered about the lives of the older staff. Miss Warburton wasn't the only one who was well past her prime and obviously unmarried. Miss Parnell from the school office was another one. You could see the difference between them and the teachers who were married, and it went further than a simple thing like wearing a wedding ring or using the title 'Mrs'. Miss Parnell and Miss Warburton had an air about them of life having passed them by.

The rain was getting really heavy by now, so I set off for home.

Miss Parnell and Miss Warburton were among the most inflexible staff in the school because the rules were all they had, or so Jill and I theorised one day in one of our library sessions. An English lesson on T S Eliot had put us in the mood to discuss the meaninglessness of existence, and a ticking-off from Miss Parnell about some trifle had given us the perfect example. We wondered what it must be like to be old and alone, but seeing all these ugly ducklings ripening into the full radiance of arrogant, beautiful youth. And to see it again and again in a never-ending cycle, year after year.

I'd said to Jill that if I were to end up like that, the last job I would want to do would be one that reminded me of all the things I hadn't managed to do with my life. Sometimes I wonder how I will end up, and it seems like I have an incredible struggle in front of me to get started in a life of my own. Passing exams, getting a job, all seem like huge hurdles that people seemed to expect me to leap. Why, I couldn't even get things together with Ben!

But I'd hate to end up so embittered that I resented all youth like so many older people obviously do.

I'd calmed down a bit by now. I still felt terribly ashamed but I realised I was just going to have to live with it.

Jeanette probably just misjudged things, I thought. People sometimes do. She did have a very excitable nature, after all. Perhaps she wasn't quite as mature as she sometimes seemed to be. Probably Jill and I just needed to keep an eye on her.

This is what I was thinking as I trudged home through the rain. I particularly remember what was going through my head because, unknown to me at that time, I had actually stumbled on the very thing that was wrong with Jeanette. Looking back on it now it was as if my subconscious had given me the key to the terrible thing that was happening.

TEN

I tried to forget the awful events of that afternoon. I certainly never mentioned them to Jill or anyone else; I still felt too ashamed for that. Jill once made a remark about the card but I answered noncommitally. No one else said anything, so maybe Jeanette and I had been the only witnesses. For that I was glad.

I never mentioned it to Jeanette either; in fact it was as if that afternoon had never happened. The following day in school she had been rather quiet, but that seemed the usual thing after one of her many and varied dramatic outbursts. She certainly was an enigma.

There was another strange happening a few days later. The swimathon was a couple of weeks away and Jeanette, Jill and Ben were practising hard, training two lunchtimes a week as well as in the evenings. On Wednesday lunchtime I went to meet them at the pool. The only people left were a handful of keen first-years and, of course, my three friends who spent so much time in the water they must have been part-fish.

I carefully made my way over the slippery tiles to the water's edge just as Ben came powering up the pool with easy, long strokes. He touched the edge to formally finish his length before he relaxed and looked up. His hair was plastered around his head, the random curls flattened. He looked very sweet.

'Hi,' he grinned.

Just then Jill and Jeanette came splashing up, racing each other to finish. Jill won by half a length because Ben was still in Jeanette's way.

'Ye-es!' gasped Jill, rather out of breath but still able to manage a shriek of triumph. 'It's the first time I've beaten you!'

Jeanette stood up, also breathing hard. 'You wouldn't have if this great oaf – ' she poked Ben playfully – 'hadn't been in the way.'

A worried look crossed Ben's face and he hastily apologised. He heaved himself out of the water, and then put down a hand to help Jeanette out.

'Ah, don't you worry,' she drawled, still looking at Jill. 'I'll get you next time.'

Ben helped Jill out too, and we started walking to the showers. I went and sat on a bench as Ben offered to give me a soaking.

Jeanette finished in the shower and turned to leave. The next person in line happened to be Charlotte Watling. Jeanette looked at her for a few seconds with venom before stepping aside and letting Charlotte into the shower. It was a hell of a look, but she didn't say anything.

We were wandering through to the changing area when Jeanette stopped.

'I left my towel by the pool,' she said. 'You go

on and join the others.' And she turned and went back towards the showers.

I found Jill already dressed and heading for the hairdryer. She always was the quickest person in the world at getting ready. I noticed her nose looked strangely pinched around the nostrils.

'What are you frowning at? Have I got something hanging out of my nose?'

'Well, er, as a matter of fact you have.'

Jill looked puzzled for a moment and then understanding flashed across her face. 'Oh,' she said, and putting her hand up, removed something flesh-coloured.

'What is that?' I said in disgust.

'Nose clip,' said Jill, massaging some life back into her septum. 'It stops the water getting in.'

Jeanette came back past, heading for a changing cubicle.

'Yeuch,' I said.

Jeanette looked over my shoulder at the revolting object in Jill's fingers. 'Oh, do you wear yours to go out?' she said sweetly, and disappeared into a booth as Jill raised a hairbrush to throw it at her.

Jill began to comb her hair.

And then froze, as I did. A scream rang out through the building, full-throated and terrified, and amplified by the resonant surfaces of the walls. Another followed it, and another. Different voices took up the wail until it became like an inhuman siren of pure terror. It was coming from the showers.

Dreading what we would find, Jill and I hurried in its direction. The pool attendant slammed her hand down on an alarm button and hurtled over from her guarding position.

Charlotte Watling was lying on the floor, drenched in blood. Her blonde hair was matted with it, dark red and sticky-looking, and her whole body was running with it. She wasn't moving.

I felt sick and had to look away. I heard Jill almost choking behind me.

When I looked again Charlotte was starting to stir. The shower was still running and some of the blood was being washed away down into the drains. A few of the girls saw it swirling towards their feet and leapt out of the way like cats so that it wouldn't touch them.

Charlotte's eyes snapped open and she began to sit up. She looked momentarily befuddled as a lifeguard arrived and knelt down beside her.

'Don't try to move,' he said briskly. 'Do you feel any pain? Don't shake your head, just say yes or no.'

Quite a lot of blood had washed off her by now, leaving her arms and legs tinged a faint orange colour. It was washing out of her black swimsuit in red torrents. Charlotte managed to bleat, 'No,' in answer to the lifeguard's question.

'But, Charlotte, your hair!' squealed one of the other first-years near by, hiding her face in her hands.

Charlotte put her hands up to her head and encountered matted, congealed sticky stuff. As she moved her hands the water washed the red down her front like a macabre hair dye. She screamed and sank back again, lifeless.

By this time the pool attendant was ready with a stretcher. She nodded to the lifeguard. 'Any injuries?'

Then she noticed a shower-gel bottle that had rolled away into the drain and picked it up. Its lid was off and a sticky red substance had started to ooze out and was slowly congealing. She snapped the lid back on and looked angrily around at the assembled crowd.

'Whoever did this is going to have a big cleaning bill,' she snarled. Everyone quailed, but no one so much that they looked like they had anything to hide. 'This is a very sick idea of a joke.'

Charlotte was coming round, so the pool attendant and lifeguard helped her to sit up.

'All right, you lot,' said the pool attendant. 'Wash off that stuff and then get into the changing-rooms.' Her voice rose. 'Quickly now! Somebody help this girl get herself in a presentable state.'

A few of Charlotte's friends gathered round and tentatively poured shampoo into her hair, squirming as the foam boiled up in a tomato colour. Charlotte started to cry. The pool attendant and lifeguard straightened up and began to take the stretcher away.

'This is going to the police,' said the pool attendant, checking the lid on the polluted bottle of shower gel was on tightly.

Jill and I met Ben outside the boys' changing rooms. He'd seen what had happened.

'Where's Jeanette?' said Jill.

We looked around and I noticed a lonely figure sitting outside on a stone wall. 'There,' I said.

We went out and joined her.

'Did you see what happened in there?' said Jill.

'Yeah,' gulped Jeanette, looking very sick. 'I couldn't watch.' She jumped down off the wall. 'We're late for maths.'

The school was buzzing with gossip all afternoon. Charlotte had to be sent home – she was unharmed, but shaken enough that the teachers decided she wouldn't have been able to endure the inevitable questioning.

A culprit hadn't been ferretted out by the end of the afternoon; the staff nevertheless put the blame on the first-years. Thankfully they considered us 'too grown up' to have been involved.

I went home, keeping my suspicions to myself.

Jill rang me later. 'It was pig's blood,' she said straight away. 'That's what the police said.'

'Oh my God,' I replied. 'How would anyone get hold of that much? There was loads.'

'Beats me,' she said.

'Well, what are they going to do?'

'Probably nothing. They'll just leave it to the school.'

'Listen, Jill, this is just between you and me but I don't think it was a first-year that did it,' I said. There. It was out before I could hesitate.

'What? Well, who was it? One of the boys?'

'I think it could have been Jeanette.'

There was a crackle of laughter at the other end of the phone. I could feel my case weakening even before I had begun.

'Why?' she said incredulously.

'No, you're right,' I said hastily. 'It's just that she went back to get her towel and – '

'Have you gone loopy? She wouldn't do a thing like that. Anyway you saw how she was outside – she turned white at the sight of blood. I know she's a bit strange but there's nothing nasty about her.'

The valentine episode was still preying on my mind too much for me to be able to tell Jill about it, and thus throw some light on what Jeanette was capable of. Especially not over the phone. I let it drop.

'Anyway,' she was saying, 'I didn't ring to gossip about school. I wanted to sound you out about going somewhere on Saturday, since it's the start of half-term. How about going to visit Tentreddon Castle? My dad got some free tickets to use there before the end of the month and he can't use them so he offered them to us. They've got a boating lake with an island in the centre, a grotto, a big house . . . It should be good fun.' Her tone became firm. 'And you could definitely do with cheering up after the last few weeks – it'll stop you imagining things! What do you say? Do you think your parents will let you come?'

I laughed. Jill was always trying to mother me. Next she'd be mentioning Ben.

'And we'll see if we can pair you off with Ben in the grotto,' she chuckled.

'Don't you dare,' I responded indignantly, then laughed. 'Yes, that's a brilliant idea, I'd love to. I might even be able to get Mark to drive us there. I'll just go and ask if that's all right. Hold on.'

He agreed, and I happily told Jill. We rang off and I felt a lot better.

The trip sounded like a wonderful idea. Little did any of us know that it was going to turn out to be anything but relaxing.

ELEVEN

On the Friday before the boat trip we were messing around as usual at lunchtime. There was no swimming practice and as it was raining outside we were hanging around our corner of the lockers.

'So tell me, Jill,' said Jeanette, 'will you be taking your nose plug on the boat with you tomorrow?'

'Why surely,' responded Jill in a put-on posh voice. She pulled the revolting little thing out of her locker and put it on. 'No well-dressed swimmer of the period was seen without one.' She took it off again and reverted to her normal voice. 'Just how do you manage to swim without one? It's so uncomfortable.'

'I'd swim without one for a date with you,' said a voice behind us. It sounded like the unnaturally deepened tones of Guy, and indeed it was. He sidled up to Jeanette.

Jeanette gave him a look of disgust. 'I really hate it,' she said, eyes narrowing as she addressed us but pointedly ignored him, 'I really hate it when someone has obviously been listening in to your conversation.'

72

We laughed. Guy looked awkward and Jeanette turned to her open locker.

'Sorry,' he said. He put out an arm to the locker and leaned on it, trying to get a bit closer to Jeanette by cutting us off. She tried to ignore him.

He looked around her locker door. 'I wonder what I can tell about you from what you've got in there?' he said.

Jeanette shot him a fearsome look. If I were him I'd have known not to carry on.

'Mmm,' said Guy, peering closer. 'Very interesting.'

'Get lost, Guy,' said Ben. 'She's not interested.'

Guy seemed to take this as an extra challenge. Why is it that some blokes just will not take no for an answer? Anyway, he moved around so that he was in front of the locker, and Jeanette immediately sidestepped to move away from him. He reached inside.

'Ah, we have a scarf, the usual books, an itty-bitty little swimsuit . . .' He whipped out the garment by its shoulder straps and it danced around like a ghost.

Ben got up and snatched it away from him. 'Just get lost, Guy, OK?' He gave the swimsuit back to Jeanette.

Guy looked as if he had been about to give up but then he took one last look into Jeanette's locker and saw . . .

'Oh look,' he said. 'Great-granny's precious mirror.' And he reached for it.

Jeanette rounded on him. 'Don't you touch that,' she said in a voice that was mostly a snarl.

73

Guy gave a horrid smile. 'Oh yeah?' He made as if to grab it and Jeanette lunged for him. Just at the last moment he pulled back, like a child teasing a smaller child. He laughed.

Jeanette's face turned to thunder. Ben came towards Guy as he lunged in again, highly amused by the way he'd got Jeanette wound up.

'Just stop it, Guy!' I called, but no one took any notice.

Guy snatched at the mirror one more time and Jeanette hurled all her weight against the sharp locker door. It slammed tight shut on Guy's hand, which immediately spurted blood. He roared like an animal.

As the locker door swung open again he was in so much pain he wasn't able to yell at Jeanette to call her all the obscene names under the sun, but that was plainly what he wanted to do.

Jeanette's face was still murderous and Jill and I pulled her away, while Ben tried to hustle Guy out of the locker room. The fingers on his right hand were bleeding profusely and one of them looked like it was nearly hanging off.

'And when you come back you can clean off the mess you've made on my locker!' shrieked Jeanette as Ben got Guy out through the door and found someone to escort him to the nurse.

'Jeanette, you sure don't do anything by halves,' breathed Jill.

Jeanette stared through the doorway, her eyes

narrowed and malevolent. There was no trace of the girl who had supposedly been overcome by the sight of blood in the showers. 'No,' she rasped softly.

TWELVE

Saturday dawned bright and sunny. Although still winter it was the clear kind of day that made you feel like being outside. I got up, excited at the prospect of our trip. Jill was right – we all needed to get away and do something different.

I hammered on Mark's door to make sure he was awake. A sleepy voice answered and I yelled that it was nine o'clock. From within came more groans and some creaks from the bed as he hauled himself out.

Downstairs Mum was already bustling about – she'd been having to get up early ever since Charlie was born. But I was surprised to see Jill already there, looking rather tired.

'Oh God, did I tell you eight-thirty instead of nine?' I gasped.

Jill smiled and shook her head. 'No, I arrived early.' She took a sip of coffee. 'I'd been awake for hours and decided to go for a walk.'

'She was walking past when I went to put the rubbish outside,' said Mum, pouring herself some coffee and passing me the jug. 'I was rather surprised – it was about seven-thirty.'

I practically spluttered into my coffee. 'And you've been down here all the time! What have you been doing?'

'Well, I've had rather a lot of breakfast.'

A stomping on the stairs announced that Mark was coming down.

Jill leaned over the table and spoke in a low voice while Mum dealt with Mark's complaints of no socks. 'Actually,' she said, 'I had this awful dream. I must have eaten something that disagreed with me, but it really was eerie. Like I was suffocating. And after that I couldn't get back to sleep. I've never really had nightmares before.'

Someone tapped on the kitchen window. Jill looked around first and raised an eyebrow. Ben was outside, with Jeanette. I waved at them to come in.

'Oh, and Sam can't come,' said Jill in a more normal voice as Ben opened the back door. 'His parents won't let him because his grades are bad.'

'Oh, shame,' I said. I tried not to take too much notice of the fact that Ben and Jeanette had turned up together.

Jill wasn't quite so delicate. 'Fancy you two turning up at the same time,' she giggled mischievously.

Ben went pink. 'We, er, just met on the way,' he stammered.

'Ah, you're too easily embarrassed,' laughed Jill. 'Like Dianne.'

I had been about to protest but instead turned

pink myself. Realising I had proved her point I turned even more red.

Mark was gulping down some cereal and washing it down with coffee. He stood up. 'You lot ready? I'm supposed to be at Chris's by ten.'

Mark had got his confidence back completely after hitting Bubbles and made good time to Tentreddon. He pulled up into the gravel drive and braked with a flourish.

'Right. I'll pick you up here at four.'

We piled out and he took off, wheels spurting small stones behind them.

'You've got the tickets, Jill,' I said. 'Lead the way.'

On the other side of the entrance gate was a long drive leading to a large house. Smooth lawns rolled away on either side, broken only by large clumps of rhododendron and other large squat leafy bushes that my mother would know the name of but I didn't. It was really quite warm, and after our walk to the house we had to take off our jackets.

Jeanette started to skip and, slightly intoxicated by this unexpected early spring, I joined in. Soon we were all galumphing through the sunny gardens like young kangaroos, oblivious of the disapproving stares from parents with younger children. We stopped by the bird house to get our breath, and leaned against one of the huge cages helpless with laughter. Eventually we noticed the birds had fled to the back of the cage

78

and were looking distinctly uncomfortable, so we thought we'd better stop.

For a while we explored the bird collection.

'They all seem to be parrots,' I said as we came across yet another creature with a hooked beak and bright plumage. 'The only difference seems to be their colour,' I said as the bird hastily made for the safety of its nesting-box.

'That one's not a parrot, it's a cockatoo,' said Jill scornfully. 'Can't you tell the difference?'

'Actually, no,' said Ben. 'We don't have long enough to look at them before they disappear off into those holes in the wall.'

'Poor things,' I said. 'I'd have thought they'd be used to people looking at them by now.' I watched as Jeanette wandered on ahead to look at some toucans. Immediately there was panic in the cage and the birds raced for safety.

I wandered up to her.

'They shouldn't be shut in cages,' she said wistfully.

I grabbed her collar. 'We're not going to set them all free,' I said only half in jest, and steered her away.

Ben and Jill caught up with us. 'There isn't much to look at here,' said Jill. 'Who wants to go and see this grotto before it gets too crowded?'

'Yeah,' we all chorused, and set off down the path again, this time at a more gentle pace.

The grotto was a mound of earth about a metre and a half high. A narrow path led to iron railings and a gate in the side of the mound. Five stone steps led down to a small archway. We ducked through one by one and found ourselves in a creepy, dark chamber with water glistening on the rocks and dripping from the roof. We stopped for a moment to allow our eyes to adjust after the bright sunshine.

'Oh, look,' said Jill. Opposite us an animal mask was carved in the wall and pale blue light shone through where its eyes, nose and mouth would have been.

'I think we can look through it,' she said.

We all went closer and picked a hole to look through. Inside was a small chamber containing three plaster masks, strange and ghostly in the pale blue light. One was smiling, one was scowling and one had no mouth.

'Weird,' said Ben.

There were more steps leading down into the earth. The ceiling above us curved up like a cave, and set into the walls were the skeletons of small animals.

'This place looks like one of those caves where you find dinosaurs,' said Ben.

'Except these look like deer,' said Jill.

'It's probably where the lord of the manor buried his faithful hounds,' I said.

The steps curved round and down and soon the roof opened out into a dome – presumably the mound we had seen from outside. The ever present sound of running water became much louder and its source was now revealed as a waterfall, coming from a large mask high in the wall and splashing over rocks to cascade into a half-circle of a pool. In the eyes, nose and mouth of the mask, as in the smaller mask above, light was visible.

'Ooh, the pool's got mirrors in the bottom,' said Jill.

We all went and had a look at our reflections in the pool and in the broken pieces of mirror cemented into its floor.

'That's a lot of mirrors,' I said. 'Someone must have had a lot of bad luck.'

'Some of them must be very old,' said Jeanette, reaching in with her hand to make swirls over her reflection.

We turned around to explore the rest of the chamber. Opposite the mask was a semicircle of wall, with three arches set into it. In each arch was a figure, life-sized and like something out of Grimm's fairy tales. The arches were outlined in shells and the figures inside were wearing a mixture of Grecian robes and fishing nets, and carrying tridents. They were painted in a ghostly mixture of greens and blues and looked like Greek goddesses that had been dredged up from the deep. In the blue-green light that suffused the grotto we all looked a little like them.

'Wow,' said Jill. 'I want to be buried in a place like this.'

'You ghoul,' I said.

More animal skeletons pointed the way out through another archway to the right of the room.

'It goes even further,' said Ben, leading the way.

Steps led down again to another chamber under the first one. It had more masks on the wall, this time lit from inside with red. One contained a treasure chest spilling gold coins over the sea-bed, and another was a fabulous array of shells, starfish and a skull.

A couple of children came clattering past, followed by their mother who was trying to look in the little grottoes while telling her offspring not to run.

We carried on along a corridor, finding similar delights through more peepholes, including one that contained an enigmatic-looking stringed instrument made from a turtle shell and a piece of driftwood inlaid with more shells and mother-of-pearl.

Finally we crossed a threshold that consisted of a pentagram inlaid in white stones. Ahead was the staircase up to daylight.

'Devil worship,' said Jill with a shiver.

'Not necessarily,' said Ben. 'It depends on which way up the pentagram is.'

'Is that the harmless way up or the dangerous way up?' I asked.

'It's the right way,' he smiled. 'And it's not harmless, it's meant to be a protection against demonic possession. The demons get upset and show their true nature.' Jill and I must have looked impressed because he smiled shyly and added, 'At least I think that's what it does.'

We headed up the steps, leaving the strange grotto behind.

Once outside we were about to head off towards the boating lake when we noticed Jeanette wasn't with us.

'She must still be in there,' said Ben.

We sat down on the grass and watched a few people come slowly out.

'What was that?' said Jill, suddenly sitting bolt upright.

'What?' I said.

'Listen,' she hissed.

From deep within the grotto we could hear screaming. It was coming closer.

A woman leapt to her feet and started to run over to the exit. 'James?' she called uncertainly.

The screaming carried on. It did sound like a child. 'James!' cried the mother, in considerably more distress. She sprinted for the grotto exit.

Everyone had scrambled to their feet as the sound of feet clattered on the steps of the grotto. A twelve-year-old boy came running out at breakneck speed, arms flailing and his face red from screaming. Tears were splashed across his face and his eyes were huge with terror.

His mother grabbed him and at first he didn't recognise her and screamed anew.

'James!' she cried, panic rising in her voice. 'What's happened?'

The boy struggled some more and tried to carry on running. His mother had to shake him. He finally realised it was her and stopped trying to escape, instead subsiding into hysterical crying.

'James!' said his mother, shaking him again. 'Tell me what's wrong!'

'It was horrible,' sobbed the boy. 'I saw a thing and it was horrible.'

His mother pulled him tightly towards her.

'There, there,' she soothed. 'What was? Was it something in the grotto?'

But the boy would not be comforted so easily. 'No, it was a thing. A real person.'

There were footsteps on the stairs from the grotto. Everyone went silent as they waited to see who would appear.

It was Jeanette.

We rushed up to her. 'Did you see anything down there?' I asked, and added a quick explanation of what had just happened.

Jeanette looked slightly sheepish. 'Well, actually, I thought it might be a bit of fun to stand next to one of the statues,' she said with a touch of shame in her voice.

A look crossed the mother's face that was somewhere between relief and anger. She looked down at her son. 'It was just a lady you saw down there,' she said firmly.

'No, it wasn't,' replied the boy, and began to cry again.

'Yes, it was,' said his mother. 'She's just come out and told us it was her.' Her voice had an edge to it that suggested what she would have liked to do to Jeanette if she hadn't had to calm her son down first.

'No, it wasn't,' he insisted.

The mother took the boy by the hand and turned him to face Jeanette. 'Now take a good look at her,' she said.

James did.

'I'm sorry,' said Jeanette, a little awkwardly.

'It wasn't you,' said James.

84

'Oh now, don't be silly,' said his mother.

'No, it wasn't,' he insisted. 'It was old and horrible.'

'Maybe there was someone else down there,' said Jill.

James's mother looked at Jeanette. 'Did you see anything?' Her voice had relaxed a fraction.

'No,' replied Jeanette, mystified. 'There was only me.'

We had watched the exit for a while and nobody else had come out.

'An old person might have fallen over,' said Ben. 'Maybe one of us should go down to look.'

By this time a man in uniform bearing a Tentreddon Castle badge was hovering around. He said, 'I'll go down and check.'

A few moments later he came out again. 'There's no one at all down there,' he said. 'Is everything all right now?'

'Yes, thank you,' said the mother. She looked down at her son. 'Perhaps you're a bit tired,' she said, and began to lead him away. 'We'll go and have a sit-down. You were probably just frightened by one of the statues or the bones.'

'I'm not frightened of those statues or the bones,' responded James through tears of indignation. 'I did see something. It was really horrible and old. It had cracks in its face and looked really evil . . .'

'But there was just me down there,' said Jeanette to us as they disappeared. 'I didn't do anything, I just stood there and he started screaming.'

Knowing her previous form I wouldn't have been surprised if she had pulled a prank and it had gone wrong, but it wouldn't have been like her to conceal the details. If she said she just stood there that's probably what she did. In that case, how did she scare the boy so much?

THIRTEEN

Ben looked at his watch. 'If we've finished scaring the other visitors we'd better go and hire our boat.'

There was a general murmur of agreement and we went back to the footpath, where we found a sign to the boating lake.

Fortunately there wasn't a queue and we were able to get one straight away.

'Is it possible to swim in the lake?' asked Jill.

'Oh yes,' replied the woman as she gave us our change. She was handsome and rugged-looking, and dressed in jeans and a navy blue pullover. 'Come this way and I'll show you to your boat. You'll be the first swimmers of the season,' she continued.

'You're mad,' I said to Jill.

'Oh, not at all,' said the woman. 'I often like to have a dip. You've chosen a nice day for it; it's pretty cold earlier in the year but now it's just beginning to warm up.'

'Great!' grinned Jill, her eyes glittering with enthusiasm. 'What do you think, Ben?'

'Definitely,' he responded.

'The boat's all yours for two hours,' said the

woman, moving back towards the ticket office. 'Have a good time.'

'Four of us, two oars,' said Ben. 'You three step in and I'll push us off.'

We got in and Ben started to push. He burst out laughing as we almost lost our balance and had to sit down.

'Haven't any of you ever been in a boat before?' he chuckled.

There was a low chorus of 'no' as he took a giant stride from the shore and got in.

'Then I'd better row to start with,' he said, reaching for the oars.

'Oh no, you don't, you male chauvinist,' said Jill, and lurched for them herself. 'Dianne, you take the other one.'

Ben watched with an amused expression as I manoeuvred into the left-hand oar seat next to Jill.

'Ready?' she said. 'One, two, three . . .'

We started to pull, but both at different times. Then we synchronised a bit more and started to move out into the lake.

'Of course,' said Jeanette, regarding us critically, 'we are going to end up going round in a big circle.'

'That doesn't matter if the lake is smaller than the circle,' I retorted, slightly puffed.

We made good time into the middle of the lake. 'OK, you lunatics,' I said, putting down my oar. 'Where do you want to take your bracing dip?'

Jill shipped her oar too and the boat drifted a

little. She looked around. 'Well, we're not too far from the island, so we could start right here.'

'We could even have a race,' suggested Ben. He looked towards Jeanette. 'What d'you think?'

Jeanette put up a hand. 'Actually, I'll give it a miss,' she said. 'I'm feeling a bit off-colour.'

I hadn't noticed it before but she was.

'You're not seasick, are you?' said Jill, looking at her with some concern.

'No . . . at least I don't think so.' Jeanette waved at Jill and Ben dismissively. 'You two go on ahead. We'll be at the island soon anyway.'

'Er, forgive me for asking this,' I said, unable to resist a smile. 'But what are you two going to wear for this little excursion?'

Jill grinned and pulled her top off over her head. She was wearing a black halter-neck swimsuit underneath her clothes. 'I came prepared,' she said. 'My towel and a change of clothes are in my rucksack.'

I was secretly glad that Jeanette wasn't going to be showing off her petiteness in a swimsuit.

'I came prepared, too,' said Ben, and also began to peel off layers. He seemed a little embarrassed while he was doing it and I didn't quite know where to look either. But when he had stripped down to his bathing shorts I remember thinking how nice it would be when summer came and he always dressed like that.

To stop myself staring at him too much I put my hand in the water to test the temperature. 'Brrr!' I said, exaggerating only a little. 'Rather you than me.'

Jill ignored me and spoke to Ben. 'Say you give me ten seconds' head start? And we'd better get in first because if we try diving from this thing Jeanette and Dianne will be swimming as well.'

Ben nodded and we braced ourselves as he eased his way over the side and into the water. Then Jill followed. Once in there they trod water with brisk movements to keep warm.

'Shall I start you?' I said. 'I've got a second-hand on my watch.'

Jill nodded. 'I'm ready.'

'OK. Three, two, one – go!' She was off and Ben looked at me waiting for his signal. Then he was swimming after her with long, easy strokes.

I sat down again in the boat. 'That looks like a long way to swim,' I said and took up the oars again.

Jeanette's answer was barely a murmur. I looked up and saw she was sitting with her arms wrapped around her as though she were very cold, and was staring into the water.

'Jeanette, are you all right?' I asked gently.

She looked round. She was deathly pale again, like I had seen her before, and her lips were a deep blue-purple. 'Yes,' she said weakly. 'I'm fine.' Then she turned away and looked down into the water again.

I carried on rowing, feeling rather awkward. What could I do? She said she was OK. What should I say next? 'Jeanette, you look so awful – I know there's something really wrong, now why don't you tell me what it is?'

As if reading my thoughts she said, 'I'm just a little tired, that's all.'

'Just say if you want anything,' I said, and then felt rather foolish. What on earth could I get her on this boat? Come to think of it I felt downright uncomfortable in her company that day.

Ben and Jill were lengths ahead of us, so I decided to concentrate on getting the boat to the island. Jill was still ahead, but it didn't look like Ben was trying to race her. Perhaps the cold water was sapping their strength.

I rowed steadily and Jeanette stared into the water as if mesmerised. That was when it started.

I had been getting quite hot rowing and was thinking about taking off my jumper when an icy wind suddenly blew over the boat, carrying with it a strange smell. The nearest thing it reminded me of was my grandmother's old powder compacts, musty and cloying. Then the freezing sensation passed.

At that moment I heard a strangled-sounding cry and a lot of splashing. I looked up and saw Jill lurch up in the water with her arms beating helplessly before disappearing under. Then she came up again, trying to scream and yell, but her cries were often cut off by the water.

I started rowing as fast as I could, and Ben sprinted towards her. He reached her and tried to take hold of her, but she was thrashing wildly and nearly pulled him down too.

I pulled the oars back and forth as hard as I could, shrieking, 'I'm coming! I'm coming!' I looked over my shoulder to see what was happening in the water.

Ben was dragged down, right under this time. He surfaced again, gasping and spluttering, but he didn't let go of Jill. I had nearly reached them by now and he finally managed to pull Jill free of whatever had got hold of her. Breathless and with our hearts hammering from panic, we managed to haul Jill into the boat and Ben climbed up afterwards.

He flopped down exhausted but was able to lift his head and speak within a few moments.

Jill was not.

FOURTEEN

She lay there in the bottom of the boat, quite unconscious.

Ben and I sat there in silence for a few minutes, saying to each other, 'She'll be all right in a minute. She's got a pulse; she's still breathing. She must have fainted.' We seemed to repeat this to each other on average every thirty seconds. Jeanette sat huddled at one end of the boat, looking shocked and withdrawn.

After five minutes we realised Jill wasn't going to wake up. 'Perhaps we'd better straighten her out,' I said. 'Isn't there a recovery position?'

'Or maybe it's better not to touch her,' said Ben. 'In case we make any injuries worse. We had a hell of a struggle out there.' He moved over to take the oars.

We changed places and I rummaged in Jill's bag and pulled out her towel. 'We'd better keep her warm,' I said, and began to dry her off. I looked over at Ben. 'Aren't you cold?'

He was trying not to show it but his teeth were chattering as he pulled back on the oars with strong, measured strokes. I picked up his jumper and threw it to him. He put it on quickly.

I put Jill's other clothes on top of her and then there was nothing else I could do but hold her hand. I glanced at Jeanette, who was still wrapped up in her own dark thoughts. Her face had an expression of deep despair. Then I looked at Ben. He gave me a quizzical raised eyebrow. I shrugged in return.

'So what happened out there?' I said.

'She must have got caught in some weeds, I guess. And they were really tough.' He looked at his arm, where a red weal was starting to look angry. 'They must have been sharp.'

'Jill's got the same,' I said. 'All over her legs.'

There was a movement behind me as Jeanette wrapped her clothes more firmly around herself. She was now staring at Jill, almost with curiosity. It was as if she had forgotten that the rest of us were there and was acting like Jill was an exhibit.

It seemed to take a long time to get back to the shore. By then the woman with the jeans and the navy jersey had seen that something was wrong and came running out to meet us.

'Quick!' I called. 'Get an ambulance!'

She disappeared into her office and then came out a few minutes later. Ben and I had jumped out on to the shore and were heaving the boat up.

'It's on its way,' said the woman. 'What happened?'

We told her, and she brought out some blankets so that we could cover Jill properly. Ben was allowed to use the office to get properly dried and changed. The ambulance did not arrive for at least twenty minutes, by which time we were frantic.

Except for Jeanette, who seemed stuck in her strange state.

'Is she all right?' asked the woman.

We nodded, but not very confidently.

'Probably shock,' said the woman.

I was standing next to Jeanette or I wouldn't have heard what happened next. The woman offered her a blanket, which she declined, graciously. Then she whispered something to herself. She only said it once, and it was very quiet. But I am absolutely sure of what she said. It was: 'Have I done this?'

Then, finally, the ambulance came. It drove down the footpath, over the grass and to the water's edge. Two paramedics got out and wheeled a stretcher over. A police car arrived at the same time, and we watched Jill being gently lifted on to the stretcher, strapped in and then taken away.

FIFTEEN

The police drove us back to town. The three of us sat in the back of the car not saying anything, while the police tried to make cheerful conversation. They seemed to think we were some silly kids who'd been messing around and had an accident. Since there was nothing we could say to convince them otherwise we didn't say anything.

They asked us where they should take us and Ben said, 'Oakhill Rise,' so we went to Jeanette's place first.

When we got there she stepped out of the car without a word and headed for her front door.

'Drugged, if you ask me,' said the policeman in the passenger seat. He and his colleague had got used to talking about us as if we weren't able to hear.

Then the driver turned to us and said, 'How far away do you two live?' He sounded fed up.

Ben replied, 'Here will do just fine,' and got out. I followed. The car drove off, leaving us standing at the edge of the road.

'They're bastards, aren't they?' I said. 'It's all a big joke to them.'

'I can't face going home yet,' said Ben. 'Do you want to come for a walk?'

I couldn't bear the thought of answering the inevitable questions at home either. We had phoned from the boathouse to ask my parents to tell Mark not to collect us, and I just knew there would be an inquest when I got home. I needed to feel calmer to deal with that.

In silence we walked to the common, and then into the shady wood that runs alongside it.

'I just want to be away from people,' said Ben.

We had come to a bench and he sat down. I sat down next to him. Then he moved closer and very gently put his arm around me, not in a pushy way, just as a comforting thing. I put my arm around him too and we sat there for a long time, hugging for comfort and rocking slightly.

It was a very nice feeling. The anxiety I had been feeling was easing and I was able to melt into the reassuring bulk of Ben's chest.

Some barrier that had been between us seemed to have broken down. It was as if we were now closer. I didn't want to spoil the silence by talking but I began to feel more and more that this was the time to tell Ben how much I liked him. But I was also aware that we were hugging like this because something terrible had happened. If I started telling Ben my feelings for him I would be taking advantage of the situation. Finally I told myself that this was not the time and the place to be thinking about my own romantic desires when a friend was gravely ill in hospital. Ben had turned to me, not Jeanette, in a distressing situation. That might mean he liked me and it might not. He had known me for longer than he'd known her, so he probably felt he couldn't just go and cuddle her while we were old friends so it was all right.

At last Ben said, 'We ought to tell Sam since we were there. Then we can explain how it happened.'

We got up and started to walk in the direction of Sam's house. Ben didn't let go of me and I was happy to walk with his arm around me. It was only when we got to Sam's place that he discreetly pulled his arm away.

Sam had already been told; Jill's parents had rung. They were also able to tell him that she was still unconscious, probably as the result of striking her head when she went under. She was in intensive care but not on the danger list. But that seemed to be of little comfort as they didn't know when – or if – she would wake up.

We went to Sam's room with him to tell him our version of events.

'I knew she wouldn't have been messing around,' he said. 'She's too good a swimmer to be silly in the water. If only I'd been there.'

'You couldn't have done anything to stop it,' I said.

He didn't answer, but got up and paced around the room. Then he said, 'Look, please don't take this the wrong way, but I think I'd rather be alone right now. Thank you for coming round . . .'

He looked up with eyes full of anguish.

I got up. 'I understand,' I said, and Ben and I went to the door.

As we went through it Sam said, 'Oh, and Ben – thanks for all you did. And you, Di.'

Outside Sam's house Ben turned to me and said, 'I suppose I'd better be going. My parents will have heard by now.'

'Yeah,' I said. 'Mine will be wanting to see if I'm in one piece too. See you.'

He turned away and then turned back again. 'I'll call round tomorrow,' he said. 'If that's OK.'

I smiled. 'Of course it is.'

'Take care now.'

'And you.'

I walked away as fast as possible. 'Take care' – he had never said that to me before. Then I told myself to stop dreaming, that love is catalysed in times when death is near. That much I had learned from the War Poets.

I found myself in Jeanette's road, and I decided to go down it in case Ben was doubling back and going to visit her. Sometimes I'm ashamed at how my insecurity makes me absurdly suspicious. As I came level with her house I could hear singing, which appeared to be coming from someone bending over in the front garden. The figure straightened up and I saw it was Jeanette, hale and hearty and energetically pulling up weeds.

'Hello,' I said uncertainly.

She leapt round. 'Dianne!' she said enthusiastically. 'How are you?'

I felt totally caught off guard. Not only was

she back to her effusive self, she was speaking in an extraordinary accent like something out of an early film. It hardly sounded like her at all. And none of my friends ever called me Dianne.

'Just thought I'd see how you were,' I said. 'Have to get home.' And with that I scurried past. I couldn't face coping with her in one of those moods at the moment.

I was thoroughly unnerved. What had happened to the frail person who the police took home? Were they right – was she on drugs? Or was that what schizophrenia looked like? Whatever it was it frightened me. Sometimes she was like a thing possessed.

I remembered how she had huddled there staring at Jill's unconscious form and whispered, 'Have I done this?'

I ran home.

SIXTEEN

Ben and Sam called round at about one-thirty on Sunday to see if I wanted to go with them to visit Jill. I managed to persuade Mum to let me off lunch but she insisted I have a sandwich before going out. Honestly, I didn't feel much like eating anyway, but my mother is convinced you're going to become anorexic if you miss one meal.

Finally Ben, Sam and I were walking to the bus stop.

'Have you heard anything?' I asked Sam.

'She's much the same,' he said. We were about to turn into Oakhill Rise when he said, 'Is it down here that Jeanette lives?'

I couldn't stop myself blurting out, 'I don't think we should take her with us.' They both stopped and looked at me as though I had gone mad. 'It's just that she seemed so deeply upset about it yesterday that she might find it hard to cope. We're going to find it bad enough.' I looked from one to the other, feeling that whatever I said would sound rather feeble. But I had a deep and intuitive conviction that Jeanette should not be allowed near Jill, and I would oppose her coming along no matter what.

Ben came to my defence. 'You didn't see her yesterday,' he said to Sam. 'She was practically catatonic.'

I didn't mention what I had seen later on yesterday, there seemed little point. But I realised it was at that moment that I began to think of Jeanette as dangerous.

So we walked on and caught the bus.

They let us into Jill's room. It was a shock for us all to see her like that, with tubes coming out of her and going in, and lying so still in the middle of it all. The only signs of life were on the monitors and dials around her, which flickered weakly but regularly. It seemed impossible that someone could remain motionless in the middle of all those intruding drips, tubes and electrodes.

'Go and talk to her,' said the nurse. 'Often they respond to voices they know.'

Ben and I looked at Sam and he moved forward until he was beside her. He leaned over her grey face. 'Jill?'

'You can take her hand,' said the nurse.

Sam looked down and gingerly reached for Jill's fingers, but as he raised her hand it moved the drips, so he dropped it again.

'Go ahead,' said the nurse. 'They won't come out easily.'

So Sam sat down and took her hand.

Ben turned to the nurse. 'When will she wake up?'

'I'm afraid it's impossible to tell,' said the nurse. 'Head injuries are very unpredictable.'

*

Later that day when I was back in my house there was a knock on the back door. I called, 'Come in,' and to my surprise Ben appeared.

'Hi,' I said, delighted. Then I noticed something strange about him. 'Is it Jill?' I asked anxiously.

He shook his head. 'No,' he said. But he looked like he had something on his mind.

At that moment Mum came in to feed Charlie. 'Hi, Ben,' she said cheerily. I decided that we needed to go somewhere more private, so Ben and I took some coffees up to my room.

Once we were there I said, 'What's wrong? You look like something's happened.'

He sat down on one of the floor cushions. 'Well, something a bit weird happened while I was at confession.'

I couldn't resist laughing. 'You didn't see a vision?!' He smiled, but I quickly added, 'No, go on, I'm listening.' One good thing about Ben was that he would be serious if you wanted him to be, and that was obviously what he needed from me right now.

'I'd got to the end of my confession and was waiting for the priest to speak – you know, to give out some Hail Marys – and instead I heard this awful laughing. I know it sounds silly but in those surroundings it gave me the creeps.' He looked down, a little embarrassed. 'So I got out of the confessional as fast as possible – probably with a look of extreme fright on my face and Jeanette was standing there, right by the curtain.'

At the mention of her name I felt a shiver of cold.

Ben carried on. 'She was wearing an old dress like the one she wore to Carla's party, and when I asked her what she was doing there she spoke to me in a really strange accent – '

'Like something out of an old film?'

'Yes!' Ben leaned forward eagerly. 'Has she done that with you?'

I decided the time had come to tell him all the strange things I'd noticed about her. I went and sat next to Ben on the cushions and told him everything, right from the jar of wasps, which I was now sure she had something to do with. I even told him about the shameful joke played on Miss Warburton. I knew I could trust him not to laugh at me, and when I had finished I felt unburdened.

'Creepy', he said at last. 'You know, I've always thought there was something odd about her as well. For one thing, I've never seen a girl quite so obsessed with her reflection.'

'Well, we all glance in mirrors whenever we go past them,' I said.

'But she stares. And not just in mirrors – in windows, everything. In the grotto she was staring into that pool for ages.'

'And she was so protective about that old mirror she brought into school.'

'She was even obsessed by her reflection in the lake.'

We talked for hours, piecing together every little thing we could remember about Jeanette and the odd things she'd done. Her thing about mirrors, her sense of humour that was almost madness, her violent mood swings.

'I wondered if it was drugs,' I said. 'She has these incredible highs and lows but I've seen her in a swimsuit and there aren't any marks on her. I suppose she might be using LSD or something,' I added doubtfully.

'Not all drugs are injected. Or it could be schizophrenia or epilepsy,' said Ben.

'But she seems to make terrible things happen around her. It's like she's possessed, or activating a poltergeist.'

Ben went very quiet for a moment. 'Actually there was something odd that I noticed just before Jill had her accident,' he finally said. 'I was swimming along and there was a sudden freezing wind, which chilled me all the way through – even though my body was insulated by the water. And there was this horrible musty smell, which was like the smell in the clothes' drawers of my grandmother's house.'

I felt distinctly shaken. 'I noticed it too. It could have been the smell of early blossom,' I said, but I knew what it really came from.

'There weren't any early blossoms,' said Ben. He knew too. 'And there weren't any weeds in the corner of the lake where Jill went down. There was something pulling her but when I went under the water the weeds were much further down. There was something else pulling her, but I couldn't see what it was.'

'What can we do?'

'Who will believe us?'

It had grown dark without our noticing. We had got so engrossed that I hadn't turned the light on and now neither of us dared to move. I suddenly became aware that we were huddled together, although not actually touching. It seemed very quiet.

As though it was the easiest thing in the world I said, 'Were you ever attracted to Jeanette?'

His face was all I could see. Softly he said, 'No,' and moved gently towards me. I felt a delicious frisson as his lips reached mine . . .

Terrible laughter rang out suddenly, cracking the silence like a bolt of lightning and jolting us apart like a charge of electricity. It came again, a horrible, mocking peal.

'It's outside,' said Ben. He jumped to his feet and was at the window in an instant. 'Oh my God. Look.'

I hurried to join him.

Down below, in the front garden, was a frail-looking figure, standing straight and proud and looking up into the moon. She was silent now, but was rocking gently back and forth as if the waves of terrible laughter were dying down inside her.

Ben turned around and headed for the door.

'Where are you going?'

'She never stops her old tricks, does she? I'm going down to find out what's going on.'

He disappeared on to the landing and made for the stairs as fast as possible. I followed.

Downstairs he snatched open the heavy front

door and ran out, calling, 'Right, Jeanette! What's this all – '

I heard his voice tail off. He had come to a standstill. I caught up with him, slightly breathless.

No one was there. The outside light had blinked on and we could see the front garden clearly.

'Where is she?' I said, looking around. But there was no one about. The only sound was the occasional gentle hum of a car moving a few roads away.

'Hey,' I said, fear rising in me. 'That outside light is supposed to come on when anyone comes into the garden. In fact it's so sensitive it comes on even when you only walk past.'

Ben looked back at me, his words echoing my thoughts. 'And Jeanette didn't set it off . . .'

And then the smell hit us: a sickly-sweet cloud of decay carried on the cold night breeze.

'What is that?' coughed Ben.

'I'm not sure,' I answered nervously, although I had a suspicion in the back of my mind about what it might be. I went to the spot where we had buried Bubbles. The smell grew stronger. 'Ben,' I called, feeling like I was about to faint. 'Come here.'

He was by my side immediately. I didn't dare look too closely at what was in front of me.

Jeanette had been trying to dig up Bubbles. I leaned on Ben for support as another waft of grave-stench drifted up. As it passed we became aware of another smell . . . the unmistakable stale odour of old face powder.

SEVENTEEN

Ben and I got a couple of spades from the garage and repaired Bubbles' grave. Only Dad came out to see what was going on and was quite sensible about it. As Ben was finally putting the spade down Mum called out in a knowing voice, 'What are you two doing out there? Isn't it time Ben was going home?'

'I'll see you tomorrow,' he said, squeezing my hand.

'Yes,' I said.

I watched him until his white jacket had disappeared into the darkness.

The next day I decided to do some shopping in the morning. The local department store was having a sale so I went along and had a look around. I was looking through some racks of clothes when a voice said, 'Di! Fancy seeing you here.'

I looked up, startled. On the other side of the rack of clothes was a head of dark hair framing a petite, almost oriental face.

'Found anything you like?' said Jeanette.

My first instinct was to run away. I hadn't

thought about what I'd do the next time I ran into her but I think I'd assumed I could at least avoid her.

'Do you think this will suit me?' She held up a long striped jumper. 'I was going to try it on.' She came around to the other side of the rail. 'Come on,' she said, grabbing my sleeve. 'You can tell me what you think of it.' She pulled me towards a fitting room.

She was obviously pleased to see me and I couldn't refuse to go with her without offering some explanation. We were just a couple of friends who'd met while out shopping, but the very normality of it after all the events of the last few weeks seriously unnerved me. Maybe I could sneak away while she was trying the jumper on.

We went to the fitting room and my heart started to beat faster as I anticipated my escape. Then at the last moment she looked critically down at the jumper and said, 'You know, I don't think this will look nice on me. I won't bother to try it on.' She hung it on the nearest rail. 'OK,' she said. 'What shall we look at next? I know, I need some mascara.'

She linked her arm through mine to lead me to the stairs. I shuddered, but she didn't notice. She was so close to me I could smell her lightly floral perfume.

'So, did you have a quiet Sunday?' she said. 'What did you get up to?'

'I visited Jill in hospital,' I answered through clenched teeth. 'And Ben had a peculiar experience in church.' I turned to give her a challenging stare but she didn't notice that either.

'Jill came out of her coma this morning,' she said as we reached the ground floor.

'What?' I exclaimed. 'How did you know?'

'I phoned the hospital this morning.'

'But why didn't her parents tell me?'

Jeanette shrugged. 'I guess they were going to get around to it. When I phoned she had only just woken up.'

This was really starting to scare me. I didn't like the idea of Jeanette keeping tabs on Jill like that.

We reached the ground floor and Jeanette wandered up to the first cosmetics counter – and made straight for the mirror. 'Jill's very tired, they said. But otherwise OK. No brain damage.' She didn't take her eyes off the mirror but stared into it like a cobra hypnotising its victim.

I had to change the subject. 'So what colour mascara are you after?'

Jeanette straightened up from the mirror and moved to the next counter. She ignored my question. 'I thought . . .' she said, pausing as she located another mirror . . . 'I'd take her a present.'

I blurted out, 'Jeanette, I don't think it's a good idea for you to visit her.'

She looked round at me. 'Why?'

I followed her to another counter and she stopped beside the mirror there. I struggled to think of an ordinary, presentable reason instead of the instinct inside me that wanted to scream:

'Just keep away from her!' I said. 'She's probably too exhausted to see anyone but her family.'

'Nonsense,' she said. 'Hospital is boring. She'll be glad to see people.'

She looked deep into her reflection again. That's when I started to notice the smell of old face powder mingling with the light fragrance of fresh cosmetics. It made me think of when my grandmother would show me little scarves and yellowed lace gloves in her dressing-table drawers, and everything would give off this cloying, musty scent. It always made me sad because the smell was like her youth gone stale.

'Yeuch,' said one of the make-up assistants behind the counter, leaning over her display and sniffing at a compact. 'I think some of this is a bit old.'

I caught up with Jeanette as she reached the chocolate section. She moved to a display of very expensive large boxes. 'This will do nicely,' she said, but it no longer sounded like her. It was that strange, clipped, old-fashioned voice I'd heard her use after the accident.

Then, tucking the box under one arm, she marched out of the shop.

I ran after her. 'Jeanette, you forgot to pay!' I gasped as I caught up with her outside.

She looked around at me with a cold smile. Her perfume had completely disappeared and now she smelled only of ancient make-up. She answered me in that same odd voice. 'I know. Do you want to help me get a few more things for Jill?'

I managed to stammer, 'No thank you,' but she was already walking away down the high street.

Then I was seized by panic and ran to a phone box to call Ben. We had to stop Jeanette getting to Jill.

EIGHTEEN

I was shaking so much it took me a few goes to get the money into the slot.

'Ben, is that you?'

A faint voice said yes. Another voice was also speaking on the line.

'I can hardly hear you,' I said. 'It's me, Dianne. There's a crossed line.'

Ben's voice said he could hear me loud and clear and asked what was wrong. The other voice, meanwhile, was making some arrangement to meet someone.

I hurriedly explained and asked him how fast he could get to the hospital. Then I couldn't hear his reply as the other voice gave a volley of instructions, ending with the words: 'We can arrange the wreath.'

'Ben!' I almost screamed. 'I can't hear you. Meet me at the bus stop for the hospital. As quickly as possible. If you can do that yell "yes" as loud as you can.'

I heard him yell, just as the other speaker was talking about cremation. I slammed the phone down and turned and ran all the way to the bus stop.

The bus was due any minute but the traffic was quite congested. I watched with ever-mounting panic as the cars crawled by.

Finally the bus came. I got on and tried to calm myself as it went up the high street centimetres at a time. But even when we were free of the traffic I couldn't shake the feeling that something terrible was about to happen.

When the bus reached the hospital stop I leapt off and looked around. The bus pulled away leaving me standing there – me and no one else. I was alone. Ben was not there.

I walked up and down. With all the delays, he should have been there before me. Hadn't he heard me? Was it the mysterious voice on the crossed line that had answered my question, not Ben?

Was I going to have to face this alone?

Surely something hadn't happened to Ben? Now I was afraid something might happen to everyone who knew Jeanette.

Then, in the distance, I saw a figure cycling up the hill, and very fast. It came closer and, to my relief, it was Ben, standing on the pedals with his legs pumping up and down like pistons and his face red with exertion. I waved madly and he managed a grin before concentrating on the steepest part of the climb.

He had just reached the more level part of the road a few metres away from me when a red car came surging up the hill and swerved towards him.

'Ben!' I screamed. 'Behind you!'

He looked round and, just in time, put on a burst of speed and veered on to the pavement. The red car swept past in an arc and barely reduced its speed as it disappeared into the hospital road.

Ben came to a shaky halt and almost fell over. I reached out to steady him.

'Crazy driver!' I shouted.

Ben was staring after the car. 'It was Jeanette,' he said, getting his breath back. 'It's her parents' car.'

'What?' I exclaimed. 'But she isn't old enough to drive!'

'No, but she's obviously got a head start on us,' answered Ben. 'Come on!' He started to run with his bike up the lane to the hospital and I floundered along beside him.

'She's going to have an accident,' he gasped. 'She can't possibly know how to control that car!'

It seemed to take an eternity to reach the end of the road, but finally we came to the little community hospital buildings and the blue rack of signs pointing to the various departments.

'Accident and emergency, orthopaedic,' read Ben. 'Where is she?'

I looked straight past the signs to a door that had a red car sprawled across its entrance.

'There!' I said, setting off at a run again. Ben ditched his bike next to the car and followed me into the antiseptic-smelling corridor. Our feet clattered as we ran to the end of it and found a T-junction.

'Can I help you?' called a voice behind us. We turned around to see a nurse sitting at a desk in an alcove.

'Could you tell us where to find Jill Casey?' I asked, trying to sound calm. 'She was in intensive care but she might have been moved.'

'She's in Room 5, Ward 4C, but I'm afraid visiting hours are nearly over.'

'Oh, please, can we just see her for a few minutes?' My calm was rapidly starting to evaporate.

The nurse took a firm tone. 'Miss Casey is only allowed one visitor at a time,' she answered, and went back to her paperwork.

'I'll stay outside,' said Ben.

The nurse looked up again and regarded us severely. 'Miss Casey already has a visitor with her,' she said.

I gave up trying to do things legitimately. I turned around and started running down the corridor as if the hounds of hell were after me.

'Hey!' called the nurse, running after me.

'Her life is in danger!' I called back at the nurse. 'That visitor will kill her!'

I didn't slow down. I took the stairs two at a time and found myself in a room with wards leading off it. By pure luck one of them was 4C.

People were catching up with me. I flung myself down the ward, which had cubicles leading off it. I reached number five.

The door was open. Through it I could see Jill's bedside table and the box of chocolates that Jeanette had stolen this morning. The lid was off.

116

I stumbled into the room. Jill was writhing on the bed, struggling to breathe and clawing at the air. Her eyes were wide and implored me to help. She had been poisoned.

NINETEEN

I ran to her. She was trying to make small noises in her throat, like an animal in pain. I felt more panic than I've ever felt in my life.

'Don't try to talk,' I gasped. 'I'll just find the alarm and then everything will be all right.'

I could hardly see straight and in the end just pressed every button I could find again and again. And I started screaming, 'Help! Help!'

In no time at all the room was filled with people. I hadn't even noticed Ben arrive but he was in the corridor when I was herded out, as a resuscitation team got to work on Jill. I leaned against Ben, trying to calm down. He was saying things to me but I could hardly hear them. All I could pay attention to were the bumps and strident commands from beyond the partition.

'Pulse is dangerously high.'

'Probably a household poison. Suggest you give activated charcoal and gastric lavage.'

And it was then that I heard a horrible laugh in the corridor.

Blind with rage, I wrested myself free of Ben's grasp and set off in pursuit. I saw a figure disappearing down to the end of the corridor and into a lift that was standing open. I arrived as the doors were closing, shutting away Jeanette's coldly triumphant face. I hammered on the lift buttons but could only watch as the lights slipped down the floors and into the basement.

With renewed vigour I pummelled the lift buttons. 'You bitch!' I yelled. 'You think you're going to get away with this?'

A nurse began to bustle towards me, obviously intent on restoring the peace. Ben was close behind her, trying to explain what had happened but without much success.

The lift doors opened behind me and I leapt in. I stabbed the 'close door' button and then the one for the basement.

Leaving the lift was like going back in time. I knew that the old part of the hospital was used as a medical museum but I had never been in it before and the contrast between it and the bright, clean world above was quite unnerving. I stepped out of the lift and looked around me. There were even cobwebs.

Then I heard laughter up ahead. I rushed on, passing large glass cases with jars containing eerie preserved remains: a tumour, a deformed foot, a hand with six fingers . . . Yellowing charts on the walls showed human blood vessels and nerves like wiring diagrams.

I reached a stout wooden door. The sign on it said 'Operating Theatre'. I heard muttering from within and an intense cold came over me. I had to make myself push open the door.

To my surprise it opened silently and smoothly

on well-oiled bearings. It was dark, with just a little light filtering in from windows set high up near the ceiling. What little light there was reflected off rows of highly polished and bizarrely cruel-looking instruments arranged neatly on trays and trolleys around the theatre. I shuddered.

It took me a little longer to see that Jeanette was in the room. She had been still as a rock but now she began to step slowly around the room, prowling like a tiger. A wave of that musty powder smell reached me and I felt sick. I looked away for a moment.

When I looked back I saw that she was carrying that old mirror of hers and talking. At first she talked softly but gradually the volume increased until I could make out that there were two distinct voices: the voice she normally used and that cracked-sounding one. Then I began to be able to make out words – only one or two at first, then whole sentences.

'I've had enough of being carried around,' said the hideous voice crossly. Although it was coming out of Jeanette it seemed strangely detached from her.

'Shall I put you down, then?' she said in her real voice. By contrast she sounded very quiet, like a child trying to please an adult.

'I have strength now,' she said in the first voice, as though she had received no answer. 'Here! Here will do!'

Jeanette knelt down and set the mirror carefully against the wall. But as she took her hands away it wobbled and she shrieked, 'No! No! I'm falling!' Jeanette caught it again, her actions gentle and quite unlike the commanding tones she was producing.

'Stand me up properly,' she said.

Jeanette found an old cardboard box and used it to steady the mirror. Then she moved back.

She said quietly, 'Is that better, Great-grandmother?'

I could hardly move. Was this the ghost of her ancestor who died in the flu epidemic of 1918?

And then something started to grow out of the mirror. At first it was a pale-coloured fog, but then it began to take shape. The smell of old face powder became overpowering, and the fog settled into areas of light and shade to reveal a terrible figure I had seen before – in a shop window and on a road at night, and probably what that little boy saw in the grotto.

This time it was even more clear. It was beyond oldness. It was a face that would make you forever frightened to grow old.

Jeanette recoiled slightly, and tried not to show it. Fortunately the hag was looking around the room. I shrank back against the door, hoping to conceal myself.

'I have enjoyed myself today,' said the hideous voice, still using Jeanette's body. 'I have done things I could never have done when I was alive! Oh no, they wouldn't have been allowed then!' It laughed. 'In my day ladies had to behave themselves. Can you imagine what it was like?

121

You are so lucky; you can act on impulse, do as you please . . .'

The voice laughed again and the terrible face made grotesque contortions. I suddenly saw the resemblance between them. She must have looked just like Jeanette when she was younger.

The face suddenly straightened to seriousness. 'You are so lucky,' it said, still through Jeanette. 'You think you have all the time in the world.' She gave another laugh: short this time, and bitter. 'Not like me – struck down by a filthy foreign disease. And I had to watch all my friends die first. I was barely older than you are now . . .' Sadness crept into her voice. 'Do you think that's fair?'

Jeanette shook her head. 'No,' she said in her real voice.

'I have been waiting for so long for this chance,' she continued as the old woman. 'Can you imagine the years going by, each one the same? Never being able to be at peace because I was wiped off the earth before I had ever really started my life?'

Jeanette shook her head again. She seemed nervous as she said, 'You've been around all that time?'

The voice gave a scornful snort. 'The dead don't just disappear conveniently,' it exclaimed. 'Not if it isn't time. We're tied here. I am tethered to the place I died; to the attic in that house where you found the mirror.' It seemed to go off into reverie for a moment. 'Ah, that mirror . . . They knew it was my favourite object. I used to love to look into it and watch my face transform as I put on powder to go out. Even after my son was born . . .' Then the creature seemed to remember where it was. It took in a deep breath through Jeanette. 'I have had to wait so very long for you.'

Jeanette's real voice asked quietly, 'Why were you waiting for me?'

The voice rose to a shriek. 'Because I couldn't live in a boy!' It lowered again and took on a horrible sincere note. 'And you were the first girl who was my direct descendant. You are of my flesh. It has taken some time for me to become powerful enough to speak to you properly but you've known for some time that I was there.'

Jeanette was looking down at the wooden floor. 'I don't know . . . I just had to do things . . . I didn't know why. But I did feel something was with me.'

'And we had such fun, didn't we? At the party, remember? I was living again. And when I am a little stronger I can live again properly. We can have a wonderful time. All the time.' Jeanette's mouth was starting to curl in distaste as she said these words; as if they were being forced out of her against her will. The hideous figure was starting to move its lips along with Jeanette's. 'You and me.'

As the creature's words passed through her Jeanette tried not to say them, like someone who has been forced to tell a lie against their will. The creature realised she was resisting.

'What's wrong, Jeanette?' it said, adopting a

mothering tone. 'You wouldn't deny me a bit of life when you have so much? After all, if it weren't for me you would not be here at all.'

Jeanette was silent for a moment and then said, 'But you made me do some terrible things . . .'

The creature's voice rose to a howl. 'How do you think I feel, deprived of life for so long? Waiting has left me bitter and frustrated. It has coloured my judgement.' The voice subsided again and became low, persuasive. 'But if you will grant me life I will be fulfilled. We will not be destructive.'

Jeanette said nothing.

'Just think,' continued the voice, 'you'll never be alone.'

Jeanette looked up sharply. I noticed for the first time that her eyes were bright with tears.

'You're afraid of being alone, aren't you?' it said. 'And you're shy – you don't have to be.' The figure started to shuffle forwards.

Jeanette's face screwed up to stop the tears that abruptly ran down her face.

'If I am with you,' said the voice, 'you will always have someone to take care of you.'

The figure inched forwards again. 'Come to me, child,' it said.

TWENTY

Jeanette was holding on to reality by a tiny thread. The figure held out its arms in a horrible parody of the way adults invite children to run to them. She must not reach her, I decided. But what could I do?

I looked wildly around. Should I break the mirror? There were plenty of heavy instruments lying about on their gleaming trays. But the creature had stepped out of the mirror and looked as if it were free of it.

'You and I,' the creature was saying. 'Two young, beautiful girls . . .' It chuckled. 'I have beauty secrets that will make you irresistible . . .'

She was nearly touching Jeanette. But even without laying a hand on her she was managing to drain the girl's energy.

I lurched forwards, grabbing one of the trays. Instruments slid off it and hit the floor like a rain of nails. Jeanette looked round at me but hardly comprehended I was there. I tried to push her out of the way but she was rooted to the spot so I held up the tray against her chest like another mirror.

'Let's see how beautiful you are these days, you old hag!' I yelled.

I waited for the scream.

None came.

'It seems we have been disturbed,' said the creature primly, still looking at Jeanette, holding her mesmerised with the dark slits that were her eyes. 'And without even knocking.'

My heart was hammering fit to burst. I had counted on shocking her into retreat. Of course, how stupid of me to assume that old trick would work.

The sound of the swing doors being pushed open alerted me. A male voice said, 'What the – '

Suddenly the place was flooded with light.

And that's when it happened.

Even I hadn't realised how terribly the old hag had aged in her grave, but what I saw in the blaze of light nearly sent me mad. The contact with Jeanette was lost, the creature looked at its own reflection properly. I shielded my eyes and then threw myself to the floor as the thing let out a horrible inhuman scream – the terrifying death-cry of a creature that had been waiting for its chance for almost a century. I dimly heard a shattering noise and suddenly shards of mirror were raining down. I curled up into a tight little ball, shrinking away as I anticipated that any moment I would feel a jagged piece enter my back like a dagger.

Then the clamour quietened down again, like a storm passing. A gentle hand touched my back instead of a sharp shard of glass. I looked up into the face of Ben.

Nurses came clattering in through the door. I

looked around me. There were no shards. There was no hideous figure that belonged to the grave. There was just a dusting of fine glass powder over myself and Jeanette.

'Are you all right?' called the nurses.

I nodded. Two nurses went to attend to Jeanette, who was lying still and pale. When they touched her she sat up and allowed them to examine her, but she did not speak in answer to their questions.

I looked at Ben. 'Get me out of here,' I said.

He helped me to my feet and led me away. We walked slowly back through the corridor of bottled remains. The basement seemed less cold.

'Better call the psychiatrist,' I heard one of the nurses say.

'I saw it,' Ben said. He squeezed me tightly against him. 'I saw you destroy it.' He squeezed me again. His voice was shocked. 'You could have been killed.'

'It was you who destroyed it,' I said. 'You turned on the lights.'

We both had one intention – to get out of this gloomy place into daylight. We came to some stairs and began to walk up slowly.

'Tell me what happened after you put on the lights?' I said. 'After seeing her, I couldn't look.'

Ben struggled to describe what defied description. 'It was like it reflected all the creature's power back at her; like a feedback circuit. And once that was done everything turned to dust.' He squeezed me again and I returned the pressure.

We arrived at the ground floor. Suddenly I remembered how we came to be there. 'Jill!' I said urgently. 'Is she – '

Ben squeezed my hand. 'She's fine. They got all the poison out of her. She's going to be OK.'

We wandered out through a side door into a garden. It was bright with sunshine, a few buds just beginning to poke through. It was simple but beautiful; life to be savoured. And lived.

Also available in the HORRORSCOPES series

SAGITTARIUS – MISSING
23 November–21st December

Employment prospects loom on the horizon but you are right to be apprehensive. Be careful – things aren't always what they seem.

Fifteen-year-old Andrea, usually known as Andi, gets a job in a crafts shop in the shopping mall. The proprietor seems a little strange but Andi's happy enough. She does, however, feel that she's being watched and finds out that two missing teenagers had previously worked in the shop. And then, when she's working late, the lights go out. Andi panics and runs out of the shop but too late – the shopping mall's on fire and Andi is trapped . . .

1 ^

CAPRICORN – CAPRICORN'S CHILDREN
22nd December–19th January

A relative is behaving strangely but act with caution – this is a dangerous time for you both.

Jan becomes concerned about her brother, Jimmy, who seems to have become withdrawn and quiet. Then she discovers articles in his room published by the Church of Capricorn and, not wanting to confront Jimmy directly, goes to the church herself. The preacher there is a charismatic man but Jan is suspicious about the church's influence over her brother – and then she hears that the congregation plan to kill themselves in a mass suicide. Can she save her brother?

AQUARIUS – TRAPPED
20th January–18th February

An argument with someone you love brings trouble crashing down like a bolt from the blue.

Following a family argument, two teenagers, Lucy and Alan, go to the cathedral one night to explore. That same evening, their father, a pilot with the RAF, is involved in night exercises with his squadron. But something goes badly wrong; a plane hits the cathedral tower and the cathedral's bell smashes to the ground – trapping Lucy inside . . .

PISCES – REVENGE
19th February–20th March

There is a price to be paid for everything in this life and your payments are now overdue.

While slightly drunk, Danny steals a car and goes joy-riding with his girlfriend, Jo. But there's an accident; Danny hits a girl in the street but, terrified, he drives off. Jo, too drunk at the time to realise what was happening, becomes fascinated by the victim of the accident, Samantha, and goes to visit the now paralysed girl in hospital, concealing her true involvement. But then, as events reach a dramatic climax, Jo discovers too late that Samantha has a thirst for vengeance . . .

ARIES – BLOOD STORM
21st March – 20th April

Loved ones will be making many demands on you. Try to stay calm.

Jack Carter, an architect, is living with his second wife, daughter and two children from his previous marriage. His first wife and son, however, live near by and there are, inevitably, meetings between them. And then strange things begin to happen; Jon's room is trashed, the brakes on Kate's bike fail, Maggie is attacked and later loses control of the car she's driving. The situation is fraught – but what's happening and could it be something to do with someone in the family itself?

GEMINI – SLICED APART
21st May–20th June

Avoid confrontations with relatives – there could be unpleasant and unexpected consequences.

Nina has never forgiven her twin, Gemma, for being born first, believing (wrongly) that Gemma is her parents' favourite. Then Nina finds that the boy she has idolised, Daniel, has started going out with Gemma. Overcome with jealousy, Nina begins to think of ways to get rid of her sister – and forges a terrible friendship with a murderer. Will Gemma be safe?

CANCER – BLACK DEATH
21st June–20th July

The sun in Saturn suggests an ominous turn of events. The distant past may come back to haunt you and you should act with caution. A good turn may have unexpected and unpleasant consequences.

A family trip to Maris Caulfield, a village which was wiped out during the plague in the fourteenth century, turns into a nightmare for Janie Hyde. Exploring the village, she discovers a cottage bearing a plaque to the people who lived and died there during the plague years – including a Jayne Hyde. Janie starts to get 'flashbacks', going back in time to watch as Jayne Hyde's life crumbles as those around her die of the plague. But it seems that Jayne's spirit is trying to take over Janie's body and Janie's own life is now in danger . . .

Nicholas Pine

TERROR ACADEMY: THE PROM

A girl goes missing down at Thunder Lake after a graduation party gets out of hand. Now, twenty years on at Central Academy, the past is forgotten – or is it?

As Kim Wedman gets the prom committee underway, the fun turns slowly into a terrible nightmare. First it's the mysterious notes, then the murders begin. As she tracks the crimes, the full horror dawns on Kim – has the killer returned from the past?

Nicholas Pine

TERROR ACADEMY: THE IN CROWD

Sandy Freeman is editor of the Central Academy Crier. When the kids from Operation Outreach arrive at Central for an educational programme, she sees her chance for a great news story. And the in crowd sees it as a chance for some fun . . .

But the story gets hotter than Sandy bargained for when the kids start to disappear. When the first body is discovered, Sandy is on the trail . . . What sort of operation is really underway?

Nicholas Pine

TERROR ACADEMY: STUDENT BODY

Abby Wilder is a bright and popular senior, a cheerleader and straight-A student. And the victim of an attacker who clearly intended to kill her!

While the police search desperately for clues, Abby's memory of the attack fades completely. But not the strange visions that seem to be warning her: this killer has rampaged before – and is about to strike again . . .

Also available in the Terror Academy *series*

Lights Out
Stalker
Sixteen Candles
Spring Break
The New Kid
Night School
Science Project
Summer School
The Prom
The In Crowd
Breaking Up

A Selected List of Fiction from Mammoth

While every effort is made to keep prices low, it is sometimes necessary to increase prices at short notice. Mandarin Paperbacks reserves the right to show new retail prices on covers which may differ from those previously advertised in the text or elsewhere.

The prices show below were correct at the time of going to press.

☐ 7497 0978 2	**Trial of Anna Cotman**		Vivien Alcock	£2.99
☐ 7497 1510 3	**A Map of Nowhere**		Gillian Cross	£2.99
☐ 7497 1066 7	**The Animals of Farthing Wood**		Colin Dann	£3.99
☐ 7497 0914 6	**Follyfoot**		Monica Dickens	£2.99
☐ 7497 0184 6	**The Summer House Loon**		Anne Fine	£2.99
☐ 7497 0443 8	**Fast From the Gate**		Michael Hardcastle	£2.50
☐ 7497 1784 X	**Listen to the Dark**		Maeve Henry	£2.99
☐ 7497 0136 6	**I Am David**		Anne Holm	£3.50
☐ 7497 1473 5	**Charmed Life**		Diana Wynne Jones	£3.50
☐ 7497 1664 9	**Hiding Out**		Elizabeth Laird	£2.99
☐ 7497 0791 7	**The Ghost of Thomas Kempe**		Penelope Lively	£2.99
☐ 7497 0634 1	**Waiting for Anya**		Michael Morpurgo	£2.99
☐ 7497 0831 X	**The Snow Spider**		Jenny Nimmo	£2.99
☐ 7497 0412 8	**Voices of Danger**		Alick Rowe	£2.99
☐ 7497 0410 1	**Space Demons**		Gillian Rubinstein	£2.99
☐ 7497 0656 2	**Journey of 1000 Miles**		Ian Strachan	£2.99
☐ 7497 0796 8	**Kingdom by the Sea**		Robert Westall	£2.99

All these books are available at your bookshop or newsagent, or can be ordered direct from the address below. Just tick the title you want and fill in the form below.

Cash Sales Department, PO Box 5, Rushden, Northants NN10 6YX.
Fax: 0933 410321 : Phone 0933 410511.

Please send cheque, payable to 'Reed Book Services Ltd', or postal order for purchase price quoted and allow the following for postage and packing:

£1.00 for the first book. 50p for the second; **FREE POSTAGE AND PACKING FOR THREE BOOKS OR MORE PER ORDER.**

NAME (Block letters) . . . .

ADDRESS . . . .

. . . .

☐ I enclose my remittance for . . . .

☐ I wish to pay by Access/Visa Card Number ☐☐☐☐☐☐☐☐☐☐☐☐☐☐☐☐

Expiry Date ☐☐☐☐

Signature . . . .

Please quote our reference: MAND